THE MISSING SLIPPER

AN AMBER MCNEIL MYSTERY

SANDRA NIKOLAI

"You cannot know what you do not feel."
Maryn Mannes, author (1904–1990)

1

———————

The Cinderella cold case, as police investigators had dubbed it, lay within the stack of files assigned to me. Logic couldn't begin to explain why I'd chosen this one instead of any other. My choice was based on a gut feeling. These cases about missing people were like living, breathing things to me, and the Cinderella file screamed out for my help.

My gift as an empath was the main reason that Ted Tremblay, chief inspector of the Montreal Police Service, had encouraged me to accept the job as consultant in the newly established cold case unit. Better known to me as Uncle Ted, he was counting on my psychic abilities to help solve some of the hundreds of cases that spanned decades.

"Amber, it's time you use your God-given talents," Uncle Ted had said to me when he and Aunt Elaine invited me over for dinner last weekend. "The investigative unit needs a fresh pair of eyes to ensure that justice is served, and you're the perfect candidate. All you have to do is carefully consider the evidence in each file. I'm sure you'll make me proud."

Talk about pressure to perform.

Sure, the consultant position was a chance to replace my

part-time jobs with a full-time one, but I didn't feel as confident about my abilities as Uncle Ted sounded. After almost twenty-five years of living with my gift, I learned that being an empath had its pros and cons. Anyone might think that sensing the energy of a person, place, or object was cool. It wasn't. Working all day in a busy store or office where many people circulated was out of the question. Tapping into someone else's unstable emotions threw mine out of whack and triggered a panic attack. Instead, I chose online jobs, like proofreading web content and grading student tests.

Solving cold cases using my gift was completely new to me. Getting psychic impressions from the evidence in case files and interpreting them properly was serious business. The police reports were all about crimes, victims, and suspects. Accurate though gruesome stuff. What if it became too much for me to bear emotionally? What if I couldn't live up to my uncle's expectations? The last thing I wanted was to disappoint him. In the end, though, his confidence in me was so strong that I accepted the job.

Detective Lieutenant Albert Payton, my boss in the Montreal Police North Division, had welcomed me to the station earlier on this rainy June morning. His short, grizzled beard and hair stood out against his police uniform, his appearance suggesting nothing less than seasoned authority. As we walked through the open office area, I noticed that most of the staff were dressed in casual wear. I had opted for a conventional look for my first day on the job: a white shirt and dark blue jacket, my hair pulled back in a ponytail. I felt immediately out of place.

The lieutenant escorted me across the floor and along a pathway barely wide enough to walk through. Filing cabinets topped with stacks of dusty files formed a wall on either side of us. "All the city's cold case files are stored here," he said, gesturing broadly.

The air smelled of dust, mildew, and defeat. An immense

sadness swept over me, even though the sole remaining traces of the victims were typewritten files. The pathway opened up to a makeshift office. A large whiteboard was mounted on the only visible wall at the back.

"This is where you'll be working," the lieutenant said. "You'll be sharing the space with one of our officers." He indicated two desks facing each other, then motioned to the man sitting behind one of them to come join us.

My pulse raced.

Tall with dark eyes and a five-o'clock shadow, the thirtyish detective in a smart suit and tie could have easily posed for the cover of a men's magazine. I caught myself staring at him as he approached us, his toned physique evoking an image of a sleek panther, the scent of his cologne suggesting the fresh outdoors. My cheeks grew warm, and I abruptly swung my gaze to the filing cabinets.

The lieutenant introduced me. "This is Amber McNeil, the unit's new member. Amber has a Bachelor of Arts degree and a good eye for detail."

The detective nodded, as if he were waiting for more, but the lieutenant moved on and introduced him to me.

That I had to work out of a cramped storage space was an unforeseen drawback. That I had to share it with Detective Sergeant Ryan Baxter, my so-called partner on the cold case files, was another. Uncle Ted hadn't mentioned either.

The lieutenant's face beamed with pride when he shifted the conversation to Ryan's investigative experience in homicides and his studies in forensic psychology. "Ryan is heading up the new criminal profiling department that I plan to expand within the unit. Budget permitting, of course."

A criminal profiler?

Discouragement washed over me. My experience was so inadequate compared with Ryan's. How could I possibly measure up to his specialized background?

"Nice to meet you, Sergeant," I said.

Ryan managed a polite smile, then turned to the lieutenant. "I wasn't expecting to share an office with my admin assistant."

He didn't fool me. I immediately sensed his resentment about working with someone as unqualified as me. On the other hand, it wasn't as if I could defend my position. While I detested the admin assistant reference, I *was* unqualified.

The lieutenant cleared his throat. "The posting recently opened up. Amber is a psychic consultant who came highly recommended because of her unique...um...observation skills. What's important is that you both work on solving some of the eight hundred cold cases stored here."

"Eight hundred cases?" My stomach knotted.

Ryan added, "We're talking decades' worth of cases. With all due respect, Lieutenant, I'll need someone other than a psychic to make a dent in those cases."

The lieutenant shook his head. "We won't get additional resources until you show progress. If you're successful, we can ask for extra funds to add offices and staff to the unit. No results, no cold case unit."

Ryan's cheeks flushed, but he nodded in acknowledgment.

It suddenly hit me that the lieutenant had said I was "highly recommended" yet hadn't referred to me as the chief inspector's niece. Had Uncle Ted arranged for me to get the job without mentioning our relationship? If so, I intended to keep it that way. No one needed to know I was his niece. Especially not Ryan, who would resent me even more.

The two men chatted briefly about a homicide case they had worked on months ago, then Ryan excused himself. He had to meet with someone in his former unit "to wrap up loose ends."

The lieutenant led me back into the quiet buzz of the outer office. He introduced me to a handful of employees, including an information officer and a computer technician, remarking again that Ryan and I had limited staff to assist us due to budget restrictions. When the tour ended, he said, "You'll have to excuse me, Amber. I've got an important meeting this morning." He retreated to his office behind closed doors.

Back in my quasi office, I examined the evidence board on the wall. It mapped out child abductions that had occurred in the northern part of the city. The names of six victims were scrawled above the map, an arrow from each one pointing to a different area of the city. The date beside each victim signified that these police investigations had come to a sudden stop two decades ago.

Ready to dig into my first case, I looked at the dusty bankers boxes stacked next to my desk. The typewritten label affixed to each one marked the case name and number. A larger sticker in an almost illegible scrawl on one of them caught my attention. It read "Cinderella." Intrigued, I lifted the box and set it on my desk.

I removed the lid, retrieved the evidence file, and read the first investigative report. The victim's name was Vicky Johnson. She was five years old when she was kidnapped from her home one night. As I studied the photo of the little girl with long dark curls and a toothy smile, a pang shot through my heart. Who would harm such an innocent child? I checked her birth date. If Vicky had survived the abduction and was still alive, she'd be twenty-five years old today. About my age.

The report stated that Eric and Christine Johnson lived in a middle-class suburban neighborhood. Vicky was the couple's only child. Eric worked for an insurance company, and Christine was a nurse. They didn't hear a thing the night their daughter vanished. Their angst about her safety was intensified by the fact that Vicky was asthmatic.

Next was a Polaroid photo taken by forensics, its white borders yellowed with age. The crime scene evidence revealed a pink slipper trimmed with white faux fur and dotted with tiny crystals. The kidnapper had dropped it on the Johnsons' front lawn when he escaped with his precious cargo through the second-floor bedroom window.

Now I understood why investigators had tagged this case by the well-known fairy tale.

I read on. Forensics had examined Vicky's bedroom and the pink slipper for fingerprints. Tests revealed no match in Canada's AFIS—Automated Fingerprint Identification System—operated by the RCMP. Police investigators assumed that the abductor had worn gloves.

Forensics found no obvious blood spatter or trace of evidence in Vicky's bedroom other than bits of earth on the floor. Although not officially stated, it was implied that Vicky's parents and the first law enforcement officers to enter the home had contaminated the crime scene by walking through it. Any evidence samples that had been collected were considered unreliable.

I flipped to the next report. An Amber alert was sent nationwide, and law enforcement teams organized searches, but no concrete leads surfaced. Police interviewed several suspects, but again, nothing. Since Vicky's parents received no demand for a ransom, investigators determined that money wasn't the motive behind their daughter's abduction.

The years passed and Vicky was never found. With ongoing budget cuts and recent criminal cases piling up, investigators abandoned her file.

Until now.

I dug into the evidence box and picked up a bag that contained a white plush bunny with floppy pink ears. It was soiled, had a button eye missing, and had yellowed with age. Why this toy had found its way into the box wasn't documented.

As I held the bunny, I sensed a warm and comforting space, yet I couldn't explain the context. The passage of time helped to clarify the meaning behind my feelings, so I'd learned to be patient. An explanation usually arrived hours or even days later.

I returned the bunny to the box, then reached for another

evidence bag. It held Vicky's pink slipper. I braced myself for what would come next.

While I held the bag, a handful of sand slipped through my fingers. I placed the bag on my desk and stood up, prepared to clean the mess. But there was no sand. Anywhere.

I picked up the bag. A closer inspection of the slipper revealed grains of sand lodged within the crevices of the sole.

Without warning, terror shot through me, the same terror Vicky must have felt when a creepy stranger swooped her out of her warm bed that night and away from her loving parents. Although I couldn't see the abductor's face, the sense of dread that came through was astounding. He was strong and evil and very much alive. His obsession with Vicky was overwhelming, but it didn't stop there. His fixation extended to other victims.

I gasped.

My heart thumped wildly.

Black spots distorted my vision.

I dropped the slipper on my desk, then tried to catch my breath. I couldn't.

My panic grew. What if Ryan suddenly returned and found me like this? He'd think I was crazy and definitely not cut out to be part of an investigative team. He might even refuse to work with me.

My powerful gift as an empath came with equally powerful emotions, something no doubt frowned upon in police investigations, where hard facts matter, and feelings can cloud judgment. I had to at least act the part and play by the rules if I was going to last in this place.

I reached into my jacket pocket, my fingers desperately clasping the amethyst crystal. Relief enveloped me as I removed it from my pocket. Like other semiprecious stones I owned, it was a gift from Aunt Elaine. She'd assured me that the jagged cluster would provide positive energy to calm me whenever I felt threatened by overpowering emotions. Since my aunt came from a lineage of empaths like me, I trusted her advice.

"Remember," my aunt had said. "The more you believe in your gift, the stronger it will become. You'll sense the feelings and emotions of others, but as a maturing clairsentient, you'll learn to manage them and use your psychic perceptions as knowledge. One day, you might not need to rely on the crystal for calm."

I held the cluster up to the light and twirled it slightly. The sharp fragments reflected miniature beams of light that glittered with each movement. After my breathing returned to normal, I put the crystal back in my pocket.

I placed the slipper in the evidence box and moved on to the last item: a video CD. It contained an old surveillance clip from a CCTV, or closed-circuit television system, that captured images from public places. I popped it into the CD player on a nearby cabinet where outdated equipment was stored for reviewing cold case evidence.

Oh, no. The film was fuzzy. Techniques to enhance old film were available, but picking a random consultant out of the phone book wasn't the established police protocol. I'd have to go through the proper channels to find out who to contact, which meant I'd have to ask Ryan.

Doubts surfaced again. It was my first day on the job, and I already needed his help. While I was eager to prove my worth, his input mattered to me. After all, he was the expert here.

What if he thought I didn't merit the job? He'd already mistaken me for his admin assistant.

What if he didn't take my role seriously and dismissed my reactions to the evidence?

What if working here turned out to be a huge mistake?

No, I had to stop imagining the worst. I shouldn't care what Ryan thought. Uncle Ted's confidence in me was the only thing that mattered.

Above all, my uncle had opened a special door that would otherwise have been closed to me forever: I had access to the file that held information about my parents the night they were murdered twenty years ago. They'd sacrificed their lives to prevent an intruder from kidnapping me.

After a quick search, I located the file labeled *McNeil, Robert and Heather* in a stuffed cabinet drawer. I pulled it out, releasing the smell of old files that had remained unopened for too long. Based on my personal connection, my uncle would have advised me against reviewing my parents' file, but I couldn't stop myself. If there was one cold case I was determined to solve, it was this one.

I took a deep breath and prepared myself for what was to come.

I opened the file.

On the very top of the papers were crime scene photos of my deceased parents, pools of blood around their bodies. I felt sick to my stomach and turned the photos over. I didn't want to remember them that way. I quickly moved on.

I picked up a photo of my parents, Aunt Elaine, and me in happier times, taken when I was five years old. My light brown hair, which I dyed to a darker shade these days, was tied in a ponytail. A jeweled paper tiara sat on my head. Aunt Elaine and my parents wore cheery smiles as they stood over me and my glowing birthday cake. Uncle Ted had probably taken the photo. A pair of blue butterfly barrettes peeked out from under the tiara, accentuating my blue eyes. I often wondered what had happened to those hair clips.

An investigative report described how loud gunshots at two in the morning had awakened a neighbor who called the police. Although our silent alarm system had been triggered, the killer had escaped. Investigators gathered no leads after interviewing relatives, neighbors, and my parents' work associates. Fingerprints found at the scene didn't match any belonging to criminals in the national RCMP database.

The file also contained the photo of a bowl of apples on the kitchen island counter, a blood-red apple impaled by a knife blade, the wooden handle standing upright. That knife, part of my parents' butcher-block set, was the last thing I saw after a police officer wrapped me in a blanket and carried me out of the house.

I dwelled on the bowl of red apples. Strangely enough, it raised images from another familiar fairy tale: "Snow White." Was it a coincidence? Or was there another reason these tales kept surfacing in my mind?

As my adoptive parents, Aunt Elaine and Uncle Ted had supplied me with ample reading material in multiple genres throughout the years, starting with a childhood collection of fairy-tale books to rival any other. The pages had suffered the wear and tear of bedtime reading, but it didn't matter. I could recite the stories by heart.

Now I was faced with evidence in two cold cases linked to fairy tales in a twisted and baffling manner. Was the fairy-tale element in both cases actually there, or was it my imagination?

That the Johnson family had lived in the same suburban community as my family was another peculiar similarity. I was an only child, as was Vicky. Was I trying to connect the dots between Vicky's successful abduction and my failed one?

There was one important difference: My parents were murdered.

I swallowed hard as tears welled in my eyes. My parents had been the center of my universe, and I hadn't had the chance to say goodbye to them. They didn't see me grow up, and I didn't see them grow old.

"You okay, Amber?"

I shut the folder and looked up, straight into Ryan's intense brown eyes. His tall, muscular frame loomed over me.

At a loss for words, I blinked back the tears. If he hadn't already considered me as totally inadequate and unfit for the job, he surely did now.

2

———————

I rose to my feet. "What can I do for you, Sergeant?"

"It's just us, Amber. You can call me Ryan." He glanced at the bankers box on my desk. "I see you're working on the Cinderella case. Want to discuss it?"

"Sure." Unnerved, I sat back down. Had he come to terms with me and my gift, or had the lieutenant told him that my presence was nonnegotiable?

While he unbuttoned his jacket and pulled up a chair across from me, I swiftly slid my parents' file under the lid from the Cinderella bankers box I'd removed earlier.

"Why did you choose to review the Vicky Johnson case?" He dug the file out of the box.

"I was curious about the Cinderella label."

"A former investigator heard the media use it and thought the tag fit." He leafed through the reports. "It was a botched investigation from the start. Like those other cases I mapped out on the crazy wall." He gestured toward the evidence board.

"Oh. *You* put up those details? That was helpful."

"Not really." Ryan closed the file and returned it to the box. "It's my job to try to find common ground among cold cases that occurred within the same geographical area. The predators usually live within or close to the same zone as their victims. They tend to kill in the places they're most familiar with."

I shuddered involuntarily. "In the Cinderella case, he probably used a vehicle to transport Vicky and make a quick escape. What if he doesn't live in the same area?"

"It's possible. Some perps got wise to our profiling methods and stalked victims outside their familiar zones. Even so, it's rare that they operate beyond their comfort zone."

I moved on. "There's one piece of evidence that needs our attention."

"Which one?"

I held up the CD. "This one. The CCTV film is hazy. It needs to be enhanced."

Ryan shrugged. "Can't do it. It would take extra funds. The lieutenant wants to keep costs low."

"We could ask for an estimate and—"

"Not a good idea. What else have you got?"

His rapid reply was enough to give me whiplash, but I stayed on track. "There were grains of sand under Vicky's slipper. They might be connected to a sandbox."

"Like in a playground?"

"I doubt her parents would have taken their daughter to a playground in slippers. They might have had a sandbox in their backyard."

Ryan nodded. "Anything else?"

This was the moment I dreaded. I tried to sound upbeat. "When I touched the evidence, I got a few impressions."

"Impressions," he echoed, his tone lacking credibility. "You mean you had a vision?"

"Not exactly. It's a perception, like an image or thought that pops into my mind. An insight about a situation. It's hard to put into words." I shared what I'd experienced from handling the objects in the evidence box.

"That's not much to go on. Fantasy has its limits. Then you cross the line."

"Fantasy? You think I'm making this stuff up?"

He sat back and folded his arms. "Solving a case without a body as evidence is the hardest thing to do. That's why it's vital we use proper police procedures and provide solid evidence in court to back up our findings."

I didn't have to be psychic to grasp that he didn't approve of my technique. His body language confirmed it. At least he didn't dismiss my insights completely. In my defense, I said, "I appreciate the advantage of having solid evidence, but I'm here to offer information about evidence that the police *don't* have."

Ryan's eyes flickered with surprise. "So that's what the lieutenant meant when he said you had a unique way of interpreting evidence." He grew serious. "It's a given we don't often use psychics in our line of work. When we do, it's as a last option, and we don't admit it to the public. It would destroy their confidence in our investigative work."

The message couldn't be clearer. I was already a burden to him. "Are you saying you'll consider my input only if it suits your purposes?"

"No, not at all, Amber. What I meant was, we welcome all the help we can get, but we tend to view psychics with...um...a fair dose of skepticism. We have to, as I'm sure you can understand."

It was no use arguing with someone whose thinking process was based solely on logic. Besides, it was my first day on the job. There would be plenty of occasions to prove myself.

I changed the subject and focused on the task at hand. "About the three suspects in Vicky's case... We have Tony Bruneau, a child molester who served time in jail. George Simon, who was flagged by an eyewitness. Lorne Tugg, a suspect who has since vanished. They would all be in their fifties or sixties today. What specifically makes them potential abductors?"

Ryan's expression became energized as the conversation shifted to a topic familiar to his field of work. "Abductors are usually white males, thirty to forty years old. Like the age of those three suspects back then. They have a strong desire to control and may or may not have a criminal history. Sex isn't always a factor. In fact, if the abductor is a loner, he might have a poor self-image, which would account for a deficiency in his relationships, especially with women. He could also be reserved and seen by others as weird."

"How does any of that relate to child abductions?"

"We're talking about two types of criminals here: pedophiles and child molesters. A pedophile has a sexual attraction to children but doesn't act on it. A child molester does."

I glanced at the cabinets stuffed with files and cringed inwardly. "With so many unsolved cases, it seems as if abductors can easily outsmart investigators."

"Luckily, we have more high-tech help today," Ryan said. "Police investigators have coordinated support from a national RCMP computerized system called ViCLAS—the Violent Crime Linkage Analysis System. It makes it easier to track the criminal patterns of violent offenders as they move across the country and internationally. A perp's compulsion to kill can lead to stupid mistakes."

"How?"

"They don't want to get caught, but their desire to fulfill a fantasy or experience the excitement they get from riskier crimes can overpower them at times. They get careless. For example, if they need money to carry out their crimes, they rob or commit other offenses. Sometimes they get caught."

"So even minor crimes committed by serial killers can raise a red flag in the system?"

"Exactly. That's why we need to search for similar elements, or a pattern, in Vicky's file and other files to detect a common MO, or modus operandi. Abduction is about feeling power over conquering others. It's absolute selfish, narcissistic behavior. It explains why these guys can usually claim more than one target."

"As for a common MO, shouldn't I be reviewing the rest of these cases too?" I pointed to the evidence boxes piled by my desk.

"I'll save you the trouble," Ryan said. "Except for the fact those crimes occurred within the same area, there's no solid evidence to link any of them to the Cinderella case."

I persisted. "I wouldn't mind taking a look at them."

"It can take months or years to solve a cold case. We don't have the luxury of time to spread ourselves thin. We have to be thorough and concentrate our efforts on one case at a time."

I was disappointed, but his argument made sense. "Do you have any more tips?"

"In most cases regarding victims of abduction, you can study their habits, their relatives and friends, and the places they frequented to get to know them better. Some people reported missing occasionally turn out to be runaways."

"We're talking about a child. And Vicky didn't run away. She was kidnapped from her bedroom."

"Right. I was speaking in general terms." He took a moment to reflect. "One possible theory in the Cinderella case is that the Johnson home might have been known to the perp. He was neat and organized because he left no evidence behind. The parents might or might not have known him. On the other hand, there could be a connection that we haven't discovered yet."

"When will we be interviewing the suspects and witnesses in the case?"

"Well..." Ryan hesitated. "Since time isn't on our side, we have our work cut out for us. We need to interview everyone in person. Body language says a lot about them."

That much I already knew from my innate sensor. Why was he stalling? "So, when do we start?"

He stiffened. "It's in the works. Look, Amber, you can tag

along when I interview people. Just let me do the questioning. Okay?"

I understood completely. After all, it was his job, not mine. "Sure."

The lieutenant rushed in, his thick-soled shoes thumping on the wood floor. "Are you two briefed on the Cinderella case?"

Wide-eyed, Ryan said, "We're reviewing it right now. Why?"

Lines crinkled the lieutenant's forehead. "The other pink slipper popped up at the Johnson family's doorstep this morning. We dispatched forensics to gather the evidence and test for DNA. I want both of you to get over there immediately to interview the parents."

Twenty years later, a second pink slipper.

This case was anything but cold.

3

———————

Dark clouds hinted at the gloom about to seep into our interview with parents whose child had been kidnapped twenty years earlier. The irony that Vicky Johnson had lived blocks away from my old home hadn't escaped me. I felt a twinge of guilt. I could have easily been the abductor's victim instead of her.

Ryan parked our unmarked police car in front of the Johnson's two-story brick home on a street lined with tall maple trees. The house was one of those cookie-cutter models from the late 1990s with a brick exterior and a double garage at the end of the driveway. Two brick planters, each containing a wilting rosebush, bordered the front door. Was it a sign of neglect, and maybe, long-lost hope? In the driveway, two forensic ID technicians in white hazmat suits were getting into a van.

"Perfect timing." Ryan cut the engine. "They're packing it up."

We waited until the van had driven off, then walked up the stone path leading to the front steps.

Ryan scanned the perimeter of the entrance, then whispered, "No home security system. If I had a kid, it would be the first thing I would have done. So much for nabbing whoever left the slipper on their doorstep." He rang the doorbell. "The next part is always the toughest."

Anxiety swelled inside me, and my hands turned ice-cold. I'd be visiting a crime scene. At least there was no dead body.

Eric and Christine Johnson were expecting us. After initial introductions were made, they guided us into their living room but didn't invite us to sit down.

"You're telling me that police investigators haven't revisited Vicky's case all these years?" Mr. Johnson's face reddened in anger. "Why did it take a slipper to land on our doorstep to get you people to investigate our little girl's disappearance again?"

Ryan held up his hand. "We're constantly reviewing cold cases. Since this is the first development in years, we're here to get your input."

"We're extremely upset that the case hasn't been solved," Mrs. Johnson said, sadness in her pale blue eyes. "We've suffered so much, not knowing what happened to Vicky."

"My partner and I are new to the case," Ryan said. "We promise we'll review it thoroughly."

"That's all good, but you're a little late." Mr. Johnson spat out the words. "We have other people helping us now. An investigative reporter named Michael Elliott. He and his partner, Megan Scott, are following up on the case."

Stunned by his disclosure, I checked Ryan's reaction.

He ignored the snub. He took out his phone instead and tapped a note. "About the new evidence... Can either of you tell us exactly how you discovered Vicky's slipper today?"

Mr. Johnson replied, "I woke up this morning and went out the front door to water the flowers as usual. Not that it helped any." He grimaced. "Anyway, I saw the slipper on the porch. At first, I thought it belonged to a kid on the street. When I showed it to Christine, she recognized it right away."

"You're certain it was Vicky's?" Ryan asked.

"Absolutely!" Mrs. Johnson said. "It had the same white fur and crystal accents. I remember it like it was yesterday. We called the police right away."

"We're glad you did. I assure you that we'll investigate every aspect of the case in depth. While we're here, we'd like to see Vicky's bedroom. Would that be okay?"

Mrs. Johnson fixed her husband with an eager expression.

"Fine," Mr. Johnson said.

As the Johnsons led us out of the living room and toward the stairway, I glimpsed out the patio doors that opened onto the backyard. A child's sandbox by the high wood fence explained my earlier reading when I'd held Vicky's other slipper. Ryan noticed it as well and gave me a knowing nod.

Upstairs, Mrs. Johnson cast a wistful gaze around her daughter's bedroom. "We left everything exactly the way it was. It became painful to change anything later on."

The bedroom clearly belonged to a little girl. Posters of Disney movies covered pale pink walls. A jewelry box in a ballerina theme topped a white dresser. A Millennium Wedding Barbie doll, an assortment of Beanie Babies, and a pile of storybooks shared the space on a small square table. I felt as if I'd entered a time warp.

Mrs. Johnson smiled at me. "Vicky was our only child. She would have been about your age today."

A lump formed in my throat, but I returned a brief smile. Her agony was penetrating, as was the despair hanging in the air.

Ryan cut into the tense moment. "We understand the kidnapper gained access through the window in this room."

"That's right," Mr. Johnson said. "It was a cool night. Vicky suffered from asthma. We shut the window as usual to keep out the pollen. Vicky must have opened it. We didn't look in on her that night and..." His voice trailed off.

"And we'll regret it till the day we die," his wife said quietly.

Mr. Johnson's jaw tightened. "It takes some nerve to drop off

Vicky's missing slipper twenty years to the day she was taken from us. Only a lunatic would do that!"

A lunatic? Or a taunting psychopath? A shiver ran up my spine.

"It doesn't change anything." Mrs. Johnson's voice remained soft, as if she were trying to calm down her husband. "Our lives haven't been the same since that day. A year later, we held a memorial service for Vicky. Of course, there was no casket."

The anguish behind their anger and regret was weighing me down. I fingered the crystal in my pocket, willing that I could draw tranquillity from it. I needed a distraction. In the next moment, I found it.

As Ryan's attention wandered about the room, absorbing the details, I approached Vicky's bed. A beige teddy bear sat among a pile of frilly pillows. I touched the bear's head, delighting in its velvety texture. "Vicky must have been a happy child."

"Yes, she was," Mrs. Johnson said. "She liked to play with her little friends in the neighborhood, yet she was just as content to play alone with her toys. She especially enjoyed helping me bake cookies." She let out a short laugh.

I waited for Ryan to take up his line of questioning, but he didn't. Recalling his warning about interviewing witnesses, I carefully phrased my next comment to Mrs. Johnson. "Forensic investigators removed a white plush bunny from the scene. I assumed it was one of Vicky's favorite toys."

"Yes, it was." She smiled wistfully at the memory. "She took it with her wherever she went, even when she played in the sandbox out back. I had a hard time taking it away from her to wash it." Her smile faded. "The night Vicky was kidnapped, she had tucked the bunny in bed next to her like she did every night. It was left behind when..." She stopped. "Maybe forensic investigators thought the kidnapper had touched it, so they seized it as evidence."

Ryan jumped back into the conversation. "We'd like to set

up a page for Vicky on the police website. We'll add details about her physical appearance and the circumstances surrounding her abduction. We'll include links to the police Info-Crime line and relevant social media sites."

Mr. Johnson eyed him with suspicion. "Why did it take another slipper for you to do what should have been done years ago? What do you expect to achieve?"

"If the kidnapper posted a photo of Vicky as a child in a social media venue and claimed she was his daughter, someone might have noticed her. We can upload progression photos of Vicky at different ages in case someone might be able to identify her through the years. Do we have your permission to go forward with our plan?"

Mrs. Johnson's face lit up. "That's a great idea." She touched her husband's arm. "Don't you think so, Eric?"

A moment of reluctance passed before he mumbled, "Fine."

"One last question," Ryan said. "Did you have a security system installed in this house at the time of Vicky's abduction?"

"No," Mr. Johnson said. "If we had, you wouldn't be chasing a damn ghost out there, now would you?"

4

Despite Eric Johnson's reluctance to accept our help, Ryan didn't give up easily. He set out to interview neighbors in case they'd spotted someone on the Johnson property late last night or early this morning.

We spoke with a dozen residents in bordering homes. No one had seen or heard anything unusual. When we reached our last stop and knocked at an elderly neighbor's home across the street, our luck changed. He had a home security system.

As we stood chatting inside Mr. Caron's foyer, he admitted he'd viewed the previous evening's video and noticed something peculiar. "It was a little after midnight when a man walked up to the house across the street. It was kind of late for a visit, seeing as the Johnsons usually turn off their lights by eleven. After so many years living on the same street, we get to know one another's habits." He chuckled shyly, as if he'd revealed a secret. "Anyway, instead of knocking at the door, the man turned around and left. Maybe he had the wrong address. It happens sometimes."

I sensed Ryan's eagerness to move things along.

"Can we see the video?" he asked.

"Come sit down. We'll watch it on TV." Mr. Caron led the way into his living room.

The video began with a clip that spanned from his front doorstep to the houses across the street. The timestamp on the video read 12:15 a.m. A man emerged from the shadows on the left and moved briskly along the sidewalk to the right. He was slim and of average height and wore a dark hoodie, which hid his face from view. He turned onto the path leading up to the Johnson home, dashed up the steps, and leaned toward the front door. He hurried back down the path, turned left, and disappeared into the shadows.

Aside from a hunched stance, his movements were agile. I determined he was a younger man. I couldn't make out what he'd left on the Johnson's doorstep. It had to be Vicky's missing slipper.

"Let's watch for a while longer," Ryan said. "Maybe someone picked him up."

But no vehicle went by.

"Maybe he took the shortcut," Mr. Caron said.

"What shortcut?" Ryan asked.

"The path bordered by thick shrubs. Right there." Mr. Caron pointed to a spot in the video where the man had vanished.

"Does it lead to the next street over?"

"Yes."

"Would you be willing to give us a copy of this video?"

Footsteps sounded on the staircase, and a young woman popped her head around the corner. "Everything okay, Grandpa?"

Mr. Caron introduced his teenage granddaughter to us. "Melanie is visiting with me today. She's studying to be a computer systems analyst." He turned to her. "The police want a copy of a video from my surveillance system. Can you help?"

"Of course, Grandpa." Minutes later, she handed us a memory stick containing the file.

"Thanks." Ryan tucked it in his jacket.

Mr. Caron's forehead creased. "Does your visit here have anything to do with the commotion at the Johnson house today? The people in hazmat suits?"

"We're not at liberty to discuss the matter," Ryan said. "Thank you for your time."

We veered around the corner to the next street and parked. Interviews with residents revealed no surveillance cameras and no additional leads.

"Mr. Caron's video was a lucky break," I said to Ryan as we drove away.

"Only if we can identify the guy," he said. "Otherwise, it's useless. We'll ask forensics to work their magic on the video. Maybe they can enhance it without having to incur extra costs."

"The man in the video was much younger than any of our suspects. He probably wasn't even born when Vicky was kidnapped."

"He could be a messenger or a friend of the perp."

A trusted friend of someone so heinous? How terrifying was that!

Something about our visit with Vicky Johnson's parents nagged at me. I backtracked and voiced my views. "Mr. Johnson sounded so bitter. If anything, our arrival on the case should have given him renewed hope."

"According to his wife, we accomplished that." Ryan steered the car around a corner. "Keeping hope alive is vital for them. In turn, it motivates us to keep searching for answers."

"Vicky's missing slipper is a good place to start."

"We have to prove it's hers to begin with."

"Her parents think it is."

"We need hard evidence," he said, echoing his usual catchphrase. "If the guy in the video wasn't a friend of the perp, he could have been a joker who planted an identical one at their doorstep. Forensics will run tests to check the slipper's authenticity."

I held my ground. "Okay, but for now, indulge me. Let's say the slipper is Vicky's. Why would the kidnapper hang onto it for twenty years, then torment her parents by dropping it off at their home?"

"Based on what I know about abductor profiling, the perp kept the slipper as a token to revive the same feelings of power he experienced when he successfully kidnapped her. It kept his fantasy alive every time he looked at it or handled it. As for the last part of your question, Vicky's parents believe her abductor wants to torment them, but I doubt it."

"Why?"

"I think the return of the missing slipper was a celebration of sorts."

"A celebration?" Then it hit me. "Oh. Twenty years to the day."

Ryan nodded. "Exactly. The perp wanted to share his success."

I stared at him. "His success? What a sicko!"

"I know. I can't imagine the pain of losing a child to a kidnapper."

Or losing your parents as a child, I held back from saying. Above all, I didn't want him to pity me. "The Johnsons have accepted that they'll never see Vicky alive again. The least we can do is try to give them closure."

"It's in the works."

"How about getting in touch with investigative reporter Michael Elliott and his partner, Megan Scott? Mr. Johnson seemed to have confidence in them."

"I took note of it. Our schedule is tight these days, but I'll try to set up a meeting with them soon."

～

Back at the station, Ryan and I crafted a page for Vicky Johnson on the police website. We wrote up her description and the history of her abduction and listed pertinent evidence we had on file.

Nadia Paquin, a university graduate who was recently hired as information officer at the station, ensured the details were accurate and complete before posting them on the site. She added photos of Vicky as a child and a link to the Montreal Info-Crime phone number for public access. She would add new photos, links, and data to the page as they arrived and use her IT knowledge in assisting investigators to trace information on leads.

Ryan commissioned an artist to produce age-progression sketches of Vicky. It would take days or longer before they would be finalized. In the meantime, excitement mounted as the site began to materialize.

I felt a particular attachment to Vicky's case and wanted to take a more active role, like handling incoming phone calls. I could also monitor the website daily for comments as soon as Vicky's page launched. Since it was a twenty-four-seven operation, Ryan and I would have to share the task with other staff. But which staff? The lieutenant had already indicated how short on resources we were.

Even so, would I be able to handle the emotions of troubled callers?

Would they disturb me so much that I would have to abandon the task?

Would my colleagues then see me as a failure?

Ryan was tapping on his keyboard, the top of his brown hair visible behind the computer screen. I didn't want to interrupt him. It was all for the better. I needed more time to weigh the repercussions of taking on extra responsibilities before I committed myself.

The lieutenant interrupted my contemplation when he strolled in. "I want to discuss the Info-Crime line with both of you as it pertains to the Cinderella case." He pulled up a chair at my desk and sat down.

Ryan joined us. "What about it, Lieutenant?" He eased himself onto a corner of my desk while keeping a foot on the floor.

"Have you decided who will be handling the incoming calls?"

"Yes," Ryan said. "We can have rotating shifts with Nadia and two other officers in communications. That's the total number of personnel you allocated to this case."

"By *we*, I assume you mean Amber and not me." Mischief danced in the lieutenant's eyes.

Ryan gave me a dubious look. "Think you can handle calls on the Info-Crime line?"

His skepticism proved to be the deciding factor. "Yes, of course I can," I said firmly. "Why not?"

"Wouldn't you feel...overwhelmed?"

I fought the urge to object. Was he truly concerned about my reaction to callers, or did he doubt my competency?

Ryan focused on the papers on my desk. Was he trying to come up with another reason why I shouldn't field the calls?

Before he tried to discourage me again, I gathered up my most confident voice and said, "Sometimes I get impressions from voices. You never know. The kidnapper might call."

He grinned. "Aren't you pushing your luck a little?"

I played to his logic. "We both know that staff resources are limited. If we don't use all available personnel for the Info-Crime line, how else will we manage the calls?"

"That's a fact." The lieutenant rose. "Good. Then it's settled." He gave us a thumbs-up, then left.

Ryan waited until the lieutenant was out of earshot. "Okay, Amber. Here's how we're going to work it. Make sure that any information you get from callers—no matter how trivial you might think it is—makes its way to me. Don't hold anything back." He returned to his desk and his typing.

I slumped in my chair and scowled at my computer screen. He didn't trust my judgment.

I took it as a wake-up call. Ryan's doubts convinced me all the more that I could be an asset to the cold case unit if he gave me half a chance.

Now all I had to do was prove it.

5

Ryan attended a conference on criminal profiling in the afternoon. All the better. I needed alone time. We'd worked shoulder to shoulder on the Cinderella case earlier, almost instinctively reading each other's next move in the process, yet I couldn't relax.

It was all about the evidence. If we tackled every case using our own separate methods of analysis, would we be able to get the results we wanted? Or would I have to struggle constantly to have Ryan accept the value of my input?

My cell phone rang, and I answered.

"Hello, dear," Aunt Elaine's soothing voice reached me. "I called to see how you were doing."

"Oh...hi, Auntie," I muttered. "I'm doing fine."

"You sound tired. They're not putting undue pressure on you, are they?"

"Not at all. I actually worked on my first case today."

A sigh at the other end of the line. "I'm sorry, dear. I can't help worrying that you're too sensitive to deal with investigations into such sordid crimes. Your uncle believes this job will help you break out of your shell. On my part, I know how badly you can react to unpleasant situations."

My aunt's reference to incidents in my youth was getting stale. Sure, I'd tapped into the pain and negative emotions of people around me and understood their misery, but I'd tried to prevent their feelings from affecting me physically by recognizing that they weren't *my* feelings. I was still working on it.

As for breaking out of my shell? My volunteer work included reading to sick kids and ailing seniors. It enabled me to reach out to people who were less fortunate than me. I hoped I could do the same by bringing closure to families of kidnapped victims.

Yet I understood her concern. "You don't have to worry about me, Auntie."

"Do you have the amethyst cluster with you?"

"Yes, I do."

She paused. "Well then, I'll let you get back to work."

We'd barely had time to say our goodbyes when my cell phone rang again. It was Nicole Latour, a friend who lived in the same apartment building as me.

"Is this a bad time to talk, Amber?"

Her slight French accent was charming, but at this moment, it was uplifting. "Not at all, Nicole. What's up?"

"I was calling to see how you were doing on your first day on the job."

For privacy reasons, I hadn't disclosed the exact nature of my work to her. I'd told her that I was working in data collection at the police station, which wasn't exactly a lie. "It's been...hectic."

"I hope it's not stressful for you." For some obscure reason, Nicole interpreted my avoidance of crowds and busy places as an anxiety disorder. From my aversion to horror movies, she assumed that I couldn't stomach dreadful or gory details. In her mind, a combination of these would devastate me.

"Getting used to a new routine is a challenge," I said. "You know how it is." Nicole was about my age and taught first-grade students at Blessed Mary Elementary School.

"Yes, I remember how scared I was on my first teaching day." She laughed. "How about catching up this Sunday afternoon? We can relax and watch a movie."

In keeping with her theories about my various ailments, Nicole suggested quiet pursuits whenever we got together. It usually involved a low-key activity either at her place or mine. Though I trusted her, I'd held back from revealing my empathic gift to her. Aunt Elaine had repeatedly warned me about the pitfalls of sharing such private information with just anyone. Some people might think that I was weird and keep their distance, she pointed out, while others might want to take advantage of me and pester me with questions.

"A movie sounds good," I said. "It's my turn, so come over to my place this time."

Silence at the other end of the line.

"Nicole, what's wrong?"

"Remember how I told you about a strange man who stood by the schoolyard fence weeks ago?"

My spine tingled. "Yes."

"Well, he came back this week."

"Can you describe him?"

"Not really. A hoodie covered part of his face. When I started to walk toward him, he ran off. Anyway, I told the principal. She advised the other teachers to watch for any strange men who try to talk to the children." The school bell rang in the background. "My break is over. I have to run. See you Sunday afternoon."

Nicole's call amplified my interest in Vicky's case. While I waited for the report from forensics regarding the newfound pink slipper, I searched online for a style similar to Vicky's. If I could prove that the slipper recently dropped off at her parents' home was nothing more than a sick prank, the case would take a whole new direction.

My search proved fruitless. Major retail outlets displayed similar styles decorated with princesses and animal caricatures, but none matched Vicky's. The slipper left at her parents' doorstep had to be authentic. It was the logical and credible conclusion that Ryan would expect.

I didn't have to wait much longer. Forensics delivered their report before the end of the day. It confirmed that the slipper left at the Johnson family's front door was Vicky's. It had the same trace evidence as the other slipper, specifically, grains of sand in the sole and Vicky's DNA. However, no fingerprints were found, and other DNA didn't match any criminal records on file, not twenty years ago and not now. The official task of confirming the slipper's authenticity to Vicky's parents was Ryan's.

I dug out the slipper from the forensic pouch that the lab had returned with the report. If the killer had handled it, I might get a reading of him.

I closed my eyes. I instantly sensed that I was in a dark, solid structure. The air was frigid.

How peculiar.

I tried again but got the same sensation of a cold, rigid, and restrictive enclosure. A pine box? A casket?

My sense of an enclosed place couldn't relate to the memorial service the Johnsons held for Vicky years ago because there had been no casket. Was this murky enclosure Vicky's burial place?

I dismissed the idea for now and put the slipper back in the pouch. I vowed not to get ahead of the evidence. Though my interpretation might suggest a future development in the case, I had to keep it in line with the solid facts we had on hand.

Above all, I wouldn't mention my perceptions to Ryan until I could prove them. They could turn out to be wrong, and he'd have one more reason to flag my incompetence.

My thoughts turned to the abductor and the reason for his reappearance after all these years. He would have had numerous opportunities to deliver Vicky's missing slipper on any of the past anniversaries. So why now?

Had he grown more self-assured and therefore more daring than before? He was clearly taunting the police, leaving a bona fide clue as if he wanted to be found.

I was determined to do just that.

6

———————

The following morning brought new momentum to the Vicky Johnson investigation. Ryan and I were meeting with one of three suspects the police had interviewed decades ago. Enthusiasm rippled through me. It would be my first hands-on opportunity to try to "read" a suspect.

Although I'd helped Ryan to create Vicky's website and offered to field calls on the Info-Crime line, I welcomed the chance to take part in a more active search for her abductor. If I could accomplish that, I was confident I could find my parents' killer.

Yet guilty feelings surged inside me. I'd broken my own rules yesterday. I'd followed Ryan's advice regarding the second slipper instead of voicing my perceptions about it. I'd neglected to use my gift, which was the sole reason Uncle Ted had recommended me for the job.

Insecurity abruptly washed over me.

What if I shared my insights with Ryan and he determined my input was useless to the investigation? Or worse, that I was a complete fake?

What if I couldn't live up to Uncle Ted's expectations?

What if...? What if...? What if...?

No. I had to stay true to myself. It was one thing to react to impressions and quite another to be clever in interpreting them. I had to deliver reliable leads to prove that I was worthy of the job. I knew I could do it. I just had to stay strong.

Ryan cut into my thoughts as we drove to our destination in Montreal North. "Let's recap what we know about our suspect so far."

I had reviewed the file and was ready for this. "Tony Bruneau is forty-five years old and a convicted child molester. His name is in the National Sex Offender Registry, so authorities are able to monitor him. Nadia confirmed that the home address we have on file for him is current."

"Tony is out on a one-year parole after having served two years in jail for attempting to molest a young child."

"He used to read stories to kids at summer camps. That's how he gained their trust."

Ryan went on. "He's been convicted three times for molesting children and considered highly likely to reoffend. He has to adhere to the conditions set up by the Parole Board under supervision of the officer from the CSC—Correctional Service of Canada."

"Because of that, he's not allowed to have contact with children or work in jobs where children are present." I gestured toward a school ahead. "Like a school janitor, for example."

"Exactly. Booze and drugs are off-limits to him, as are dealings with shady characters. The least sign that he's involved in any type of criminal activity is bad news for him."

"What about access to social media? He can reach kids that way."

"Not a chance. Tony is forbidden to have access to the internet or cell phones without supervision. He's also forbidden to contact previous victims."

I quivered. "Who would want to hurt a child? Or snatch them away from their parents?"

"Pedophiles don't see it that way. They'd be horrified if someone thought their actions were harmful to children. When they kidnap a child, it's because they have no choice."

I stared at him. "No choice?"

Ryan nodded so-so. "It's not that pedophiles *prefer* children. They choose children because they lack the social skills to have relationships with women. It's theorized that it's part of their desire to be loved and accepted."

"That's sick."

"It gets worse. There are no housing restrictions on perps like Tony Bruneau."

"What do you mean?"

"They're allowed to choose where they want to live. In Tony's case, where he lives doesn't change his habits. His last psychiatric assessment confirmed that he remains fixated on sexually abusing young girls. Guys like him are prone to offend again."

Annoyance rose inside me. "If he's such a risk, why did they let him out of jail?"

Ryan shrugged. "He served his time. No one can hold him longer than his jail term. That's how the system works."

"I know, but it's frustrating. What do you expect to learn from questioning him?"

"He told investigators he had an alibi the night Vicky was kidnapped. The file doesn't indicate whether or not it was confirmed. I did a check, and the name of the witness Tony gave them popped up in a recent obituary."

Uh-oh. In my hurry to read the file, I'd missed following up on that detail. I'd have to be more thorough from now on.

~

The apartment block was located in a low-income area of the city. Several broken windows were patched up with wooden boards, leaving the inhabitants to fend off the wet weather, unless or until the building owner arranged for repairs.

After Ryan parked the car out front, two young boys playing ball in the street stopped to gawk at us. One boy gave the other a nudge.

"This area has one of the highest reports of assault in the city," Ryan said before we stepped out. "No one parks in this part of town unless they live here, or they're cops." He shot a subtle side-glance toward the boys. "Those kids know the make and model of cop cars. Even the younger ones have it all figured out."

A cracked stone path led to glass double doors with two tiny holes in them, probably caused by pellet shots. Inside the lobby, the wind whistled through the glass like twin teakettles at boiling point. Bordering the graffiti-plastered cracked walls, discolored laminate flooring curled from water damage. The air was filled with an odor of something long past its "best before" date.

As the elevator screeched its way up to the fifth floor, I struggled with the fact that I'd soon come face to face with Tony Bruneau, a man who had abused innocent children. How would I feel in his presence? What could I possibly say to him?

Too soon, the elevator doors parted.

"Remember, don't ask any questions," Ryan warned as we made our way down the corridor to Tony's apartment, solving one of my issues. "Just follow my lead."

He knocked on the door to Tony's apartment.

A man with disheveled hair and droopy eyes opened the door but kept the safety chain on. He snapped, "Whatever you're selling, I don't want any."

Ryan slapped a hand against the door to prevent it from closing. "Tony Bruneau?"

"Who wants to know?"

Ryan flashed his police badge at him and introduced us.

"You should have said so in the first place." Tony let us in, then stood aside and made an effort to button his shirt.

The scent of marijuana stung my nostrils. As I walked by Tony into the narrow hallway, I caught the smell of liquor on his breath.

Ryan sniffed the air. "You been smoking something?"

Tony flapped a hand in front of his bony face, then shut the door. "Nah. A friend came by and smoked a joint."

"He had a couple of drinks for you too?"

Tony said nothing. He scurried to the kitchen table and made a pretense of cleaning up. He set aside a deck of cards and a cell phone, closed a laptop, and emptied an ashtray in a wastebasket under the sink.

Ryan motioned to the phone and laptop. "Isn't your online access restricted?"

"They're from social services," Tony said, avoiding a direct answer. "I ain't doin' nothin' illegal. I'm a responsible person. I got to be. I have a puppy now." He pointed to a young golden retriever chewing on a toy bone in a corner of the kitchen. "A neighbor's dog had pups and he gave me one."

Ryan moved on to the purpose of our visit. "I want to talk to you about a cold case file. Vicky Johnson."

"Who?"

"Don't play games with me, Tony. The girl was kidnapped twenty years ago this week. The Cinderella case."

A spark flickered in Tony's eyes. "Oh...yeah. So that's what this is about." He smirked. "I already told the cops I had an alibi that night."

"Do you know anyone who can attest to that?"

"I was at a bar with a friend. Enzo Malta. Don't you damn cops take notes?" Tony glowered at him.

"Where can we find him?" Ryan asked, even though we already knew the answer.

"In the cemetery. He died two months ago."

"How?"

"He was sick and..." Tony hesitated. "He OD'd."

Ryan dug out his phone and tapped a few keys. "You been hanging around any schools or playgrounds lately?"

"What? You think I'm an idiot?"

"Don't mess with me." Ryan angrily aimed his phone at him. "You know what happens when you lie about stuff like that."

Tony clenched his teeth. "No damn way you're puttin' me behind bars again."

"I'll ask you one more time. Did you visit any schools or playgrounds recently?"

"No, I didn't." Tony folded his arms.

His defensive stance was a sign he was lying. I flinched. This grown man might have harmed another child.

Ryan's phone rang. "I have to take this call." He retraced his steps back to the hallway.

Tony pulled out a chair at the kitchen table and sat down, then grinned at me. "Oops! I forgot my manners. Have a seat." He waved toward two other chairs across from him, one of which had a jacket hanging from the back of it.

As I moved toward the empty chair, my hand brushed against the jacket. Severe pain shot through me, and I fought to contain my emotions. If my perception had a connection to Tony, why hadn't I picked it up from him earlier? Why from his jacket? It wouldn't be twenty years old, so it couldn't have a connection to Vicky Johnson. Maybe my insight represented another event in Tony's past or future. I sat down, slid a hand into my pocket, and fingered the amethyst cluster to gain composure.

Tony's expression was pinched. "I'm done with jail. No goin' back there for me. You don't know how dangerous it is in that place. Inmates get beaten up all the time. That's how I got this." He raked a hand through his messy hair and pulled it back to reveal a two-inch scar on his forehead. "They'll kill me the next time."

That Tony had suffered a beating in jail could explain my experience moments earlier. Or was it a presentiment that he would soon be incarcerated again and suffer another beating?

He ranted on. "My life is different now. Since I got out, I made new friends in a therapy group. I go to sessions twice a month. It counts for somethin', you know." He stuck his chin out, as if he'd accomplished a good deed.

I made a mental note to ask Ryan about the parole officer and Tony's participation in the therapy group.

Tony reached for the deck of cards on the table and spread it out on the table. "Been playin' this game I learned in jail. They call it Tarot or somethin' like that. I pulled up the death card this week." He showed me a card with a skeleton wielding a sickle. "People think it means death. They're wrong. It means change. Change is a positive thing. Like that pup over there." He motioned toward the puppy and grinned.

My readings of Tony conflicted. Could this man with a soft spot for a puppy be the pitiless kidnapper who had mocked police with Vicky's missing slipper?

His phone call over, Ryan rushed up to us. "Amber, we're leaving now." To Tony, he said, "We'll be in touch."

I was surprised at our sudden departure but waited until we were inside the elevator to voice my thoughts. "You hardly questioned Tony. What's up?"

"All I wanted was a recent photo of him." He showed me the picture he'd secretly taken with his phone. "It was perfect timing. The front desk received a request for officers to visit an elementary school about a block from here. They reported a strange man hanging around the schoolyard."

My breath caught in my throat. Was it where my friend Nicole taught? "Which school?"

"St. Paul Elementary."

I was somewhat relieved to learn that it wasn't Nicole's school. Not that the sighting of a strange man at another elementary school was exactly welcome news.

7

———————

Mrs. Maher, the principal of St. Paul Elementary School, reminded me of a history teacher I'd once had. Short black hair, no makeup to conceal the telltale signs of a middle-aged face, and a stiff, formal manner that discouraged foolishness.

After Ryan and I introduced ourselves to her in the school lobby, she went straight to the issue at hand. "Thank you for coming here today. We've experienced our share of concerns over the years, but this recent incident is quite troubling, to say the least. Please follow me."

We trailed her along a corridor. Nostalgia hit me as the scent of damp lockers and the aroma of chicken soup and hot dogs from the cafeteria wafted our way. Glass encasements on the walls held student photos and award plaques for achievements in various subjects, along with photos of the principal and her staff. To my relief, classes were in session, so I didn't have to worry about being bombarded by the diverse emotions of children rushing about.

Mrs. Maher ushered us inside her office. "Please have a

seat." She indicated two vinyl chairs facing her desk, then closed the door.

After she settled in a high-back chair across from us, she joined her hands and said, "As you know, we take the welfare of our students very seriously. Our teachers reinforce safety guidelines daily, especially when it comes to the younger children. We warn them about talking to strangers."

"You reported that a man had been visiting the schoolyard," Ryan prompted her.

"Yes. In fact, there were two."

"Two? Can you describe them?"

"Personally, I can't. I didn't see them. However, I can ask the teacher who did." She walked to another door that led to an adjoining office, whispered instructions to the woman sitting at a desk, then returned. "Miss Foley will join us soon." She chatted on about the weather and how the school was preparing for an outdoor graduation day ceremony that families would attend.

Mrs. Maher hid her nervousness behind a calm bearing. Based on her earlier comment, she'd weathered a number of problems at the school, yet I sensed this latest incident had affected her more deeply.

There was a knock at the office door. A young woman peeked inside, her blonde hair falling in curls to her shoulders. "You asked to see me, Mrs. Maher?"

"Yes. Please come in and close the door behind you." The principal made the introductions. "Miss Foley, these officers would like to ask you a few questions regarding the strange men you recently saw by the schoolyard fence. Please have a seat."

Miss Foley smiled nervously at us, then sat down in the vacant chair next to Ryan.

Ryan tried to put her at ease by guiding the conversation. "Miss Foley, can you start by telling us about the men you saw?"

"I saw two different men on separate occasions. Each man

stood outside the schoolyard fence and spoke to some of the younger students."

"Can you describe the men?"

She tugged on the edges of her pink cotton shirt. "I-I'm not sure. I was on supervisory duty at recess and happened to notice the first man standing there. He was thin and had dark hair. Wore casual clothing. The other man could have been heavier and older. I can't say for sure."

Ryan dug out his phone and showed her the photo of Tony Bruneau he'd taken earlier. "Does this man look familiar to you?"

Miss Foley stared at the picture. "Yes, he's one of the men I saw. I've seen him standing by the fence more than once. He was taking photos of the children with his phone."

"Recently?"

"A couple of days ago."

"And before that?"

"Uh...a week ago. Sorry, I can't remember exactly." She bit her lip.

"That's okay." Ryan slipped the phone into his pocket. "And the other man? Had you seen him by the schoolyard more than once?"

"Not really." She shrugged. "Sorry I can't be more helpful."

"You did great," Ryan said. "Thank you."

Mrs. Maher dismissed the teacher, then addressed us. "After these latest episodes, I've instructed my teachers to be extra vigilant and to caution the children repeatedly about talking to strangers who linger by the schoolyard fence. I can assure you that the children's safety is our priority." Her gaze lingered on us as if to emphasize her pledge. "Is there anything else I can do for you today?"

"No, thanks," Ryan said. "We appreciate your time."

❧

On our way back to the car, I said to Ryan, "A positive identification. This means Tony could be in deep trouble, right?"

"Eyewitness accounts aren't always accurate. But if it is Tony, he lied to us about not visiting school premises. I have to report him to the parole officer. We need eyes on this one."

I shared my disturbing experience at Tony's apartment earlier. "He told me he was afraid to go back to jail because he'd suffered beatings from inmates. I don't know if what I sensed was an event that already happened or will happen. Even so, why would Tony risk going back to jail if his life was in danger there?"

Ryan raised an eyebrow. "He might not have a choice at this point."

"What do you mean?"

"Things are adding up for Tony and not in a helpful way. If he violated his conditions, his parole officer might decide to send him back."

After we got in the car and buckled up, I mentioned Tony's therapy group. "He sounded happy to be part of that group. Like it was a positive thing in his life."

Ryan pressed his lips together. "Here's the thing. If his parole officer decides that Tony has to go back to jail, his participation in a therapy group won't make any difference." He paused. "Unless his supervisor puts in a good word for him. And even then..."

"I can't wrap my head around it. Why would Tony give up his freedom by hanging around a school in full view of the staff? What was he thinking?"

"He can't help it. Stalking kids is a tough habit to break." He steered the car down the street.

"Are you making excuses for him?"

"Not at all," he said. "It's the nature of the beast. Perps like him are prone to offend again. Miss Foley's testimony was proof that he's kept his old habits."

"How about talking to his therapy group manager? He might tell us more about Tony."

"Exactly. We might latch onto other leads there. I'll set it up as soon as I can."

That Ryan had accepted my suggestion encouraged me to ask, "What's next?"

"We'll visit another suspect in the Vicky Johnson case tomorrow morning. George Simon. Right now, I have to go to a meeting. I'll drive you back to the station first."

After Ryan dropped me off, I didn't enter the police station. I got in my car and drove home instead. I'd already cleared my schedule with the lieutenant, and he'd given me his okay to work at my volunteer jobs this afternoon.

I could have told Ryan, but I wasn't comfortable sharing my outside activities with him. It was a safeguard I set up for new people who entered my life, and it suited me fine. Until I trusted someone wholeheartedly, which was rare in itself, I kept aspects of my private life out of the conversation.

Likewise for inviting people over to my place. It wasn't because my sparsely furnished, single-bedroom apartment looked as if I were moving out instead of in. The truth was that I enjoyed my quiet space after a day's work. Best of all, everything in it belonged to me. Other than a new bedroom set I purchased when I moved in several years ago, my aunt and uncle gave me a new royal-blue couch as a housewarming gift. I'd originally bought second-hand pillows for the couch, but I kept sensing the former owner's weird vibes from them. I gave them away and ordered new ones.

The apartment was merely a stepping stone to my next goal, which was to move back into my parents' old house. No one in their right mind would consider living in a place where two murders had occurred. Then again, I wasn't just anyone.

As my legal guardian, Aunt Elaine had put my parents' house up for sale. She left the original furnishings and window dressings in most of the rooms "to increase sales appeal." But it hadn't sold. The main reason? By provincial law, the real estate agent had to disclose the murderous event that had occurred there to prospective clients. Since potential buyers were shocked at the reference to a "murder house," the prospect of selling it swiftly faded. My aunt leased out the house instead. When I turned eighteen and was barely out of high school, I couldn't imagine the financial responsibility of taking legal possession of it. So, I agreed that we keep leasing it.

When I recently voiced my desire to inhabit the old house after the lease with the current tenants expired, Aunt Elaine tried to discourage me. "The energy from the trauma is embedded there," she said. "It'll impact you negatively. Do you really want to live in a 'stigmatized property' or 'murder house,' as real estate agents call it? Besides, the income from the lessees paid for your education and so much more all these years. You can keep leasing it out, or sell it and use the money to do whatever you want."

I dismissed her excuses. I hadn't set foot inside the house since the tragic event that claimed my parents' lives, but I wasn't afraid to do so. The ambiances there would be familiar and welcoming to me.

To reinforce my goal, I often flipped through family photos to keep the happy memories alive and to visualize myself in the old house. With the salary from my new job as police consultant and no mortgage on the house, I was confident that I could make it work.

Although I could legally acquire the old house when the current lease expired, I didn't want to create ill feelings between my aunt and me. After I explained how attached I was to the house and how the move would fill a huge void in my life, she agreed. She promised to have it professionally cleaned before I moved in and handed me the keys.

All to say that I was that much closer to getting my wish.

I changed my clothes before heading out half an hour earlier than usual to my first volunteer job: reading to seniors at a local retirement home. I enjoyed seeing their faces light up on my arrival, especially Mrs. Brody on the third floor who called me a different name every time I visited her. Other dementia residents didn't acknowledge my presence or stared vacantly at the wall. It didn't matter. I sensed that they heard my words and appreciated my visits.

I'd almost reached Mrs. Brody's room when a man in jeans and a sports jacket caught my attention. He was moving rapidly toward the opposite end of the corridor and disappeared through the exit door. I didn't see his face, but I was almost certain it was Ryan. Was he following me?

No, it couldn't have been Ryan. Why would he be here? Besides, he'd told me he was going to a meeting. My mind was playing tricks on me.

Mrs. Brody greeted me with her usual sunny smile. She stood by the window, her hand on the back of the armchair. "Hello, Kathleen."

I didn't bother to correct her. Instead, I smiled. Suffering from dementia, the elderly woman with the sweet personality had already dubbed me as Jackie, Rona, Susan, and other names. The names didn't matter. What mattered was that she felt at ease with me.

We took our usual seats in the armchairs. On the small table between us was a framed photo of her with her husband who'd passed away years ago, and another photo of the couple in earlier days with their son, Dash, when he was three years old. I'd once asked Mrs. Brody if Dash was a nickname for Dashiell. She'd replied no. Her son inherited the name because he kept running into trouble before he even learned how to walk.

"What would you like me to read for you today, Mrs. Brody?" I asked.

She reached for the first book from a pile on the table. "I don't think you've read this one." She handed it to me.

"Ah! *Jane Eyre.*" I'd read the story to her many times before, but she didn't remember. I didn't object to reading pages from it again. It was worth seeing the enjoyment on her face.

Before I could finish my reading session, Mrs. Brody fell asleep. I placed a blanket over her lap and tiptoed out.

I drove to my next volunteer job. The patients in my young audience at General Hospital differed from week to week, so I didn't know who would be there to greet me.

Today I made extra time for the children who were on an extended stay at the hospital. Despite Danny's battle with cancer, Abby's recovery from a broken leg, and Karl's recent eye surgery, these five-year-old patients sat quietly while I read their favorite fairy tales out loud. Their expressive faces and spontaneous laughter filled me with happiness. It was the least I could do to try to bring joy into their lives.

On the drive back home, the memory of the children's smiling faces had me wishing I could grant each of them a fairy-tale outcome. No child deserved to suffer. Each child deserved a happy, healthy life.

While some people might view my wishes as unrealistic, though admirable, I had it within my grasp to do something tangible to ensure the safety of children. I could try to protect them from predators lurking in the shadows.

Predators like Tony Bruneau.

8

———

The weather was cooler than normal on my drive to the station the next morning. The leaves on neighboring trees fluttered in the wind, their surfaces glistening from an earlier rainfall.

My thoughts fluctuated just as wildly as I recalled our visit with Tony Bruneau yesterday. The police hadn't been able to prove he was behind Vicky Johnson's kidnapping decades earlier. From Tony's viewpoint, he had an alibi, but it was impossible to prove it. His friend, Enzo Malta, was dead, eliminating that likelihood.

Tony had spent time in jail for molesting children since then. If he'd retained his old habits, as Ryan claimed, had he committed other similar offenses that had gone undetected in the interim?

Innocent until proven guilty, I supposed.

I arrived by eight and found a note on my desk from Nadia who'd worked the night shift till seven this morning. She'd received the illustrator's age-progression sketches of Vicky and posted them on the girl's website, then launched the site to the public. Otherwise, she noted, it had been an uneventful night on the Info-Crime line.

I checked if anyone had left comments on Vicky's website. There were several spam remarks, which I promptly deleted.

There was one surprise, though: an anonymous call recorded on the Info-Crime line minutes before I arrived. Although the caller had used software to camouflage his or her voice, the message was clear. It suggested that we take a closer look at George Simon as a probable pedophile. The caller even provided George's home address.

My heart pounded. Another likely predator had been flagged, one who was already known to police. The message included a tip that put George Simon and a white van in the area of the Johnson home the night of Vicky's disappearance.

The voice was disguised, yet I sensed that the caller wasn't merely a Good Samaritan identifying a criminal. The distress in the voice signaled legitimate fear, a sign that he or she might have a close connection to George Simon.

Ryan made his way through the outer office and came up to me, disrupting my analysis. "Ready to go to our next interview?"

I told him about the anonymous call. "I could tell that the caller was afraid but left a message anyway."

He picked up the phone and listened to the recording. "Interesting. They're responding to information we released on Vicky's website."

"It's quite the coincidence."

"What is?"

"That we're about to go visit George Simon, the next suspect in Vicky Johnson's case."

"We'll find out more soon enough. Let's go." Ryan's tone was abrupt.

Something was sure bothering him.

I followed him out to the parking lot behind the low-rise

police station. I had reviewed George Simon's file and was prepared to start off the conversation this time, but an unforeseen development stopped me in my tracks. Several reporters were waiting outside the police station.

A female reporter held a microphone inches from Ryan's face. "Sergeant, we learned from the police website that you're revisiting Vicky Johnson's cold case. Do you have anything new to report?"

"Any leads on who kidnapped the little girl?" a male reporter asked.

As we brushed past them, Ryan barked, "This is an ongoing investigation. I have nothing more to say."

We hurried to the car and buckled up.

"That's all we need," Ryan said between clenched teeth. "Reporters breathing down our necks." He swerved out of the parking lot and into the traffic.

I didn't understand his anger. "They're only doing their job."

"Well, their timing sucks." His grasp tightened on the steering wheel. "Let's go over George Simon's file."

Grateful for the change of topic, I began. "Here's what we know so far. George Simon is in his fifties. He's lived in the same apartment building for decades. It's located three blocks from the school that Vicky Johnson attended."

"As for George's profile," Ryan said, calmer now, "he lacks social skills. He has difficulty befriending women and is somewhat of a loner. He used to work in delivery. A sample of his DNA and a follow-up interview back then affirmed that investigators couldn't prove a connection to the Cinderella case, though notes about his alibi are vague. This latest anonymous tip about a white van is our best lead so far."

"One more thing. If you give me a chance, you'll find that I'm quite capable of asking the right questions during a witness interview."

He mulled it over. "Okay, give it a go but tread lightly. We might be dealing with a killer who would do anything to cover his tracks, including knock off a police officer or consultant if he considered them a threat."

～

We parked in front of a ten-story apartment block that dwarfed the 1950s semidetached bungalows surrounding it. Like other rental buildings in this low-income area, its lobby had deteriorated over time. The linoleum had holes in it the size of golf balls, and the walls suffered from an overload of graffiti.

We rode the creaky elevator up to the sixth floor. Once again, my pulse increased at the thought of our impending interview. We might be standing in the same room as Vicky's kidnapper, a man who might have also attempted to kidnap me when I was five years old.

Was I exaggerating? I hadn't ever met the man, so how could I judge him? Anxiety mounting, I slipped a hand into my pocket and clasped the crystal to calm my nerves.

Ryan knocked at the apartment door and whispered to me, "Let's hope he didn't make a run for it after my phone call."

A chunky, broad-shouldered man in a stained white apron opened the door. George Simon's eyes skimmed over me and settled on Ryan.

Ryan held up his badge and introduced us. "We spoke earlier."

"You're here about the missing Vicky girl, right?"

"You got it."

A smile lit up George's round face, outdoing the shine on his bald head. "Come in."

I sensed he was a friendly type, a little on the shy side. Nothing disturbing like Ryan's depiction of a potential killer. On the other hand, I couldn't form a valid assessment at this early stage. Some people were experts at hiding the ugly aspects of their personality.

The odor of chicken soup wafted our way as George led us down the hallway and into a space that comprised the kitchen and the living room. The layout of apartments in this area were similar in the way they offered a large open area, as if eliminating an extra wall made all the difference in construction costs.

"Have a seat." George motioned toward four chairs around a round oak table. "Excuse me for a moment. I have to add veggies to the soup." He took a few steps to the stove.

While we waited, I caught a subtle movement by the living room window. Was that a cat resting on the back of an armchair? A second glimpse confirmed it was a gray-haired woman sitting with her back to us. Only the top of her head was visible until she stretched her arms out to adjust a black shawl around her shoulders.

I gave Ryan a nod in her direction.

"Hey, George," he said. "I didn't know you had a visitor."

George followed his gaze to the petite woman and acted as if he'd noticed her for the first time. "Oh, that's my mother. She lives with me."

"Since when?"

"It's going on twenty years now."

"Twenty years?" Ryan eyed him with suspicion. "You told police investigators that you lived alone when they questioned you about Vicky Johnson's disappearance."

George hesitated, as if he were trying to find a plausible excuse. "I was embarrassed," he grumbled, giving Ryan a quick glance over his shoulder. "A grown man living with his mother. A mother who had to support him financially. What would they think?"

"She could have provided you with an alibi," Ryan said.

"I doubt it." George strolled over to the table and whispered, "She was in the hospital recovering from surgery at the time."

He set his heavy frame down with a thud in a chair opposite me but looked at Ryan. "Now she's in the early stages of dementia and has no memory whatsoever about lots of stuff."

"So you're taking care of her," I said.

"I have no choice." George heaved his broad shoulders upward in a shrug but kept his eyes on Ryan. "I quit my job because Mom needs full-time care. I can't afford to put her in a retirement home. Her income and mine barely cover the rent, groceries...my meds. I suffer from high blood pressure." He sighed. "Caring for Mom is my sole purpose in life now."

Was that sincerity I detected in his voice?

"That's very noble of you, George," I said.

"You gotta do what you gotta do."

"What line of work were you in twenty years ago?" Ryan asked him.

George shifted in his chair. "General delivery."

"For what company?"

"All kinds of companies. Contract work."

"You had your own vehicle?"

"Yes. A small van."

"Do you still own it?"

George shuffled his feet. "No, I got rid of it."

"What color was it?"

"What difference does it make?"

"Answer me," Ryan insisted.

"White."

A slight moan from his mother spurred George to his feet. "Coming, Mom." He filled a glass with water and brought it to her.

Ryan stood up and followed him. "How about introducing us to your mother?"

I joined them and stood by the window, eager to see how George would react.

He grew flustered and couldn't recall our names, so Ryan made the introductions.

Mrs. Simon's smile softened the wrinkles on her face. "How nice of Georgie to invite his friends over!" To her son, she said, "Why don't you read us a story?" She pointed to a stack of children's storybooks on the windowsill.

Before George could answer, I picked up a book from the pile. The cover was illustrated with colorful baby animals.

I perceived intense fear emanating from a young girl who had held this book. She was trying to run away from a man. I gasped, hiding my insights with a cough.

Ryan caught on. "You bought these children's books for your mother, George?"

"No, they're not hers."

"Who do they belong to?"

"A lady who lives in the building." George rubbed his hands along the sides of his apron. "She's a single mother. She ditched her husband a few years back. I babysit her young daughter sometimes to help her out."

"Do you babysit children often?"

George huffed. "What are you getting at?"

"Nothing," Ryan said. "Just asking."

"This is about that missing Vicky girl, isn't it?" George pursed his lips. "Like I told the cops before, I had nothing to do with it. That same night, I was with my mother at the hospital."

"There's nothing in our investigative files about a hospital visit. Can you prove it?"

"The hospital should have a record of her stay there."

"I don't think they keep records for that length of time."

George glared at Ryan, then leaned toward his mother and put a hand on her arm. "Hey, Mom. You remember when you were in the hospital? It was about twenty years ago."

"Don't do this," Ryan cautioned him.

George's behavior shocked me. From my experience reading to seniors with dementia, I understood how they lived in their own world of memories and how confused they became when confronted with facts they'd long forgotten. George's goading of his mother's memory was beyond cruel, especially if he was lying about her stay in the hospital.

Mrs. Simon gazed up at her son. "The hospital? It was the night you were born. Such a beautiful baby." She smiled.

"Stop it, George," Ryan said between clenched teeth.

George straightened up with a grin, no doubt satisfied that he'd made his point. "The cops interviewed me and other tenants a week after the Vicky girl was kidnapped. I forgot to tell them about my visit to the hospital. It was a simple mistake. That's all it was."

"A mistake?"

"Yes. Don't make a big deal out of it." He stared at Ryan, his fists tightening at his sides.

George's posture suggested aggression, yet I detected something else: a deep-rooted anger. Oddly enough, I sensed it was about a whole other matter.

Ryan accessed his phone and tapped a key. "Give me your mother's full name and the name of the hospital where she stayed."

George complied. "Mrs. Shirley Simon. General Hospital."

"What's the name and apartment number of the neighbor whose kid you babysit?"

George's eyes narrowed. "You have no right to stick your nose in my personal affairs. What business is it of yours?"

"I ask the questions around here." Irritation filtered through Ryan's voice. "Give me your neighbor's information, or I'll drag you to the station for questioning."

"On what grounds?"

"Impeding a criminal investigation."

"Oh, yeah?"

I cut into their heated conversation. "George, there have been other kidnapping attempts in the area lately. We're interviewing parents who have young children, so it's important that we speak with your neighbor."

He looked at me, then switched his attention back to Ryan. "Her name is Berta Tole. Apartment 320."

Ryan tapped the information on his phone. "We're done here for now. We'll get back to you if we need to ask you more questions."

George walked us out without another word, then slammed the door shut behind us.

9

————————

Ryan tapped the elevator button for the third floor. "I can read you by now, Amber. What happened back there?"

"When I picked up the storybook," I said, "I had a strong sense of fear. It came from a young girl who was trying to escape a terrifying situation."

"Is that right?" Doubt seeped through his voice. "What was she afraid of?"

"Someone. A man."

As we stepped into the empty elevator, he said, "George is hiding something. That's a given. If he's our guy, he might still be victimizing children. Unfortunately, I'm going to need more than your perceptions to connect him to Vicky Johnson's case."

There was that snub again. I refused to take his remarks about my gift as an insult. "I get it, Ryan. Having solid evidence on hand is required in any police investigation. But you know what? If you gave me half a chance, my input might help you find that evidence."

He raised his hands. "Okay, okay. Did you get anything from George?"

"Yes. He's angry and frustrated. Maybe living with his

mother and having to quit his job to take care of her stopped him from achieving his own goals. He *did* say that she was his sole purpose in life."

"He could have fooled me. The way he lacked respect for her...played head games..." Ryan's jaw tightened. "It disgusted me."

His strong reaction to George's insensitivity surprised me. It meant he had compassion for the elderly. At this moment, I had the utmost admiration for him. "George's behavior was crude, but I think his mother means more to him than he lets on. Like I said, he feels he lost out on following his dreams."

"It's possible that he compensates for his loss by kidnapping little girls."

"What do you mean?"

"By abducting children, he would be fulfilling a desire to achieve a goal in life that he can claim as his personal destiny. It's all about feeling in control and getting what he wants. For him, it could be much easier to abduct kids than women."

I gave his theory some thought. "George definitely avoided eye contact with me. He seems uncomfortable in the presence of women. Except for his mother."

"You're accurate as far as reading his body language goes." Ryan gave me an approving nod.

Was that a glimmer of respect I detected?

He went on. "I liked the way you talked him down and said we were interviewing people about other kidnapping attempts. The good cop, bad cop routine."

I hadn't considered my approach in that way, but his comment was encouraging. "Thanks." His gaze lingered on me. I couldn't help sensing the strength of his character and the effect his innate charm had on me. Embarrassed about my attraction to him, I changed the subject. "Um...about George's mother. Will you be able to access her medical records?"

"Hospitals in the province aren't required to keep records

for more than ten years. I'll check anyway. There's a chance they didn't destroy them."

We headed down the corridor to apartment 320 and knocked. After Ryan held his police badge to the peephole, the sound of bolts being unlocked pierced the air.

A woman peeped through the narrow opening of the safety-latched door. "Yes?"

Ryan introduced us. "Are you Berta Tole?"

"Yes."

"We'd like to speak with you about a missing persons case. May we come in?"

"Yes." She led us down the hallway and across the kitchen. "I can only give you a few minutes. I start my shift at the diner soon."

Although her apartment had the same open layout as George's, a sofa and two armchairs cleverly separated the living room from the kitchen. The place was tidy, and stripy marks on the carpet meant it had recently been vacuumed.

Berta invited us to sit on the sofa while she settled in an armchair.

Ryan began his line of questioning. "What kind of work do you do at the diner?"

"I wait on tables," she said. "Depending on the day, I can work up to ten-hour shifts. I'm almost forty years old, but I can still run around like a spring chick." She laughed. "I also clean apartments. Whatever it takes to pay the rent."

Despite her ability to be a hard worker, or maybe because of it, Berta Tole wore her forty years in an unforgiving manner. Her wispy black hair was tied back in a severe ponytail, and bangs failed to hide the deep creases along her forehead. Bony knuckles protruded from rough hands that revealed the hours of labor central to the jobs she held.

"We just had a talk with George Simon, one of your neighbors in the block." Ryan paused to assess her reaction.

Berta's lips tightened. "So?"

"He told us he babysat your daughter."

"Not anymore."

I joined the conversation. "He has a collection of children's storybooks—"

"They're the ones I lent him," Berta cut in. "My ex-husband bought them for Ella on her fourth birthday last month." She picked up a framed photo on the coffee table and handed it to me. "This is my baby. Isn't she sweet?"

I held the photo so Ryan could see it. Suddenly the same disturbing sensation I'd experienced earlier jolted through me. I veiled my reaction with a smile and handed the photo back to her. "She's very pretty."

She put it back in its place. "Either of you got kids?"

"No," I said.

Ryan didn't answer. "How long have you and your husband been separated?"

"A few months. My ex had a terrible temper. We fought a lot. Sometimes he got violent and Ella—" She stopped. "It wasn't right to keep my daughter is an abusive relationship, so I kicked him out."

"What's your husband's name?"

"Gus. That's short for Gustave. Same last name. Tole. I haven't had the time to change my papers back to my maiden name."

Ryan tapped a note on his phone and went on. "You said that George no longer babysits Ella. Why not?"

"I found a new sitter that's better suited for my daughter."

I had to know. "Why did you leave her storybooks with George?"

"I bought Ella new books." She glanced at her watch and made a move to get up. "Sorry, I have to leave for work soon."

"One more thing," Ryan said, rooting her to the spot. "Police interviewed people in the area about twenty years ago. They were investigating the disappearance of a young girl named Vicky Johnson."

"That's the case you wanted to talk to me about?"

"Yes. Do you remember it?"

"The Cinderella case. How could anyone forget it? I was a teenager then, but it hit me hard. Even more so now that I'm a mother." Berta blinked. "Wait a minute. All those questions you asked me about George... You think he's—"

"We understand the police interviewed you back then," Ryan said.

"Yes, they did. They also interviewed my parents and everyone else in the building. Why are you questioning me again about it?"

Ryan deployed one of his detective strategies. "We recently received an anonymous tip on our Info-Crime line about a potential suspect in the Cinderella case. We have reason to believe that you might be involved."

Her expression paled. "Involved? How?"

"I'll be direct. Were you the anonymous caller?"

She blurted, "No, it wasn't me. You're mistaken. No way it was me." She checked her watch again and stood up. "You really need to leave. I have to go to work now before they fire me."

The windshield wipers could barely keep up with the downpour that had intensified since earlier this morning. Ryan said nothing and drove slowly to avoid splashing pedestrians clutching umbrellas. It was a considerate move, yet I sensed that his extended silence hid deeper thoughts.

I suspected he was as disappointed about our meeting with Berta as I was. We'd left her apartment no further ahead than when we'd first knocked at her door.

"What did you get from our interview with Berta?" Ryan finally asked.

"We scared her," I said. "I expected her to run out of the apartment screaming and leave us there."

"We definitely hit a sore spot. Her reaction convinced me that she might be the anonymous caller to the Info-Crime line. It could have something to do with George babysitting her daughter, Ella." He paused. "Anything else?"

I surveyed the steady flow of traffic in the left lane as he merged into it. "The photo of Ella... I had the same feeling about a terrified child when I held the storybook at George's place."

"Really?"

"Yes. Do you think I'm making this up?"

A twitch played on Ryan's lips. "If you're right, then we're getting somewhere. If George was responsible for Vicky Johnson's disappearance and is still preying on young kids, it means he could have been flying under the radar all this time."

"I'm not so sure."

"About what?"

"That it was George. I don't know the man's identity because I couldn't see his face."

He gave me a quick side-glance. "What? You mean you *never* see faces?"

"Sometimes I only get vague images or thoughts about people and their emotions. It's hard to interpret what I pick up because it often seems out of context. It falls into place eventually."

Ryan frowned, making no attempt to conceal his irritation. "You were saying...about not suspecting it was George?"

"Berta told us her husband bought those storybooks," I said. "She also said he was violent. Since I don't know who Ella was afraid of, it could have been her father, George, or another man."

"That totally screws up my theory. Damn!" He slammed his hand against the steering wheel.

His anger pulsated through me. "Stop it, Ryan!"

He threw a frantic look in my direction. "Hey, I'm sorry. I didn't mean to upset you."

I grasped the crystal in my pocket, annoyed that I had to rely on it to calm me down. "Go on. You were talking about your theory."

"Right. If Ella wasn't afraid of George, then Berta wouldn't have a reason to call the Info-Crime line and leave a tip about him. Which means someone else made the call."

My mind refused to move on. "What about Ella's father? Berta said he had a terrible temper. If he found out that George was babysitting his daughter, maybe he wasn't crazy about it. Maybe *he* made the anonymous call."

"There's a hitch. How would he know that George drove a white van decades ago?"

"For that matter, how would Berta know?"

"She could have lied about not knowing. I'll run a check on her husband anyway."

Soon after we arrived at the police station, Ryan asked for a search of Gustave Tole on the criminal database. Aside from a complaint from Berta about a violent incident several years ago, no charges had been laid against her ex-husband.

More news arrived from General Hospital. Their administrative offices confirmed that medical records were destroyed after ten years. It meant that George wouldn't be able to prove his alibi.

Despite the setbacks, Ryan's mood lightened up. "Without proof that his mother was admitted to the hospital twenty years ago, George Simon's alibi is flimsy. It's one reason to keep him on our black list."

I agreed that we shouldn't ignore George as a suspect. Yet Ryan's decision to err on the side of caution made me doubt my own abilities all the more. Added to my uncertainty were more questions that remained to be answered:

The children's storybook in George's apartment had belonged to Ella. Who was she afraid of?

Berta had claimed that her husband had been violent at times. Had he recently harmed her or Ella?

Had George abused Ella on his babysitting watch? Was it the real reason Berta had removed her daughter from his care?

Had George lied to us? Was he hiding a deep, dark secret?

My stomach churned at the horrific possibilities, but I heeded Ryan's advice not to jump to conclusions. If anything, I had to take my perceptions at face value and not read more into them than what was obvious.

Yet my emotions were torn. Although Ryan would argue that our investigation had to rely solely on the hard evidence collected, I needed to trust that my insights would add to our efforts and guide us along the right path.

If only I could stop doubting myself.

10

The pelting rain blurred my drive to work the next morning. The forecaster blamed a hurricane thousands of miles off the southern coast for the far-reaching downpour. Though heavy traffic was a daily occurrence in this city of almost two million inhabitants, the storm caused numerous accidents and made me twenty minutes late.

I barely had time to remove my wet raincoat and hang it on the rack by the crazy wall when Ryan burst into our quasi office.

"Got a few minutes?" Smiling, he held two take-out cups of coffee.

"Yes, if one of those is for me," I said.

He set the cups on my desk. "I got extra cream and sugar, in case." He dug the items out of his pocket and placed them next to the cups.

My radar was up. It was only coffee. But why this sudden show of generosity? There had to be a catch.

Ryan pulled up a chair. Handsome in a rugged sort of way, he struck me as the kind of guy that had women falling all over him in clubs, or wherever he chose to spend his nights off. My inner voice warned me to keep him at arm's length, and that was exactly what I intended to do. I never shared my private life with the people I worked with anyway. In Ryan's case, his lack of confidence in my abilities gave me no reason to form any kind of bond with him outside of work. It was strictly business between us.

Ever on guard, I sat down at my desk and poured cream into my coffee, then drank some. Whatever the blend was, it was delicious. "What's the occasion?"

"I owe you one for yesterday." Again, the wide smile.

"For what?"

"I've been thinking about your...umm...experience at George Simon's apartment." He emptied a tiny packet of sugar in his coffee. "I might have jumped to conclusions about George. After Berta Tole told us that her ex had bought Ella the children's books, my perspective changed. Ella's abuser could be her own father, not George."

"Are you eliminating George as a suspect in Vicky Johnson's kidnapping?"

"Definitely not. He hasn't come up with a solid alibi yet for the night Vicky disappeared." He drank more of his coffee. "Are you up for the next challenge?"

"Do I have a choice?"

"Not really."

Lieutenant Payton rushed into the office, his demeanor somber. "I'm glad I got you both before you left the station. I just got off the phone with the powers that be. They're reviewing our unsolved cold case stats with a focus on the next budget. Bottom line: I need to put the unit to good use ASAP if I expect their continued financial support."

"Lieutenant, we've only begun to investigate the cases," Ryan said.

"I don't doubt your commitment. However, unless there's a positive outcome on any of these cases within the next week, I'll have to cut back." Worry tightened his expression.

The next week?

If the choice came between Ryan and me, would the lieutenant favor police experience over a psychic consultant? Or would the unit be completely abolished?

"We're doing our best," Ryan said. "We're actually working on new leads."

"We promise we won't let you down," I said.

The lieutenant nodded. "That's what I like to hear. I'll try to stall headquarters before they make a final decision." He walked out.

Ryan whispered, "If there was ever a doubt about the future of the unit..." He let out a sigh of unease. "Okay. Let's discuss our third suspect in the Cinderella case."

I opened the file that had earned a permanent place on my desk and examined the first report. "Lorne Tugg was a consultant who lived blocks away from the Johnson family when Vicky was abducted. He would be fifty-five years old today."

"We won't be meeting with him because the guy has disappeared off the face of the earth," he said with a wry sense of humor. "But—and this is important—we have a witness. Her name is Kim Barley. She lived in the same apartment building as Lorne Tugg back then."

I picked up another report. "She'd be about forty-five years old today. She was the reason investigators interviewed Lorne Tugg. She lodged a complaint against him for harassment."

"Lorne Tugg contradicted her claim. He told the police she wanted to date him, but he wasn't interested. He showed the officer a photo of himself with a blonde woman, presumably his girlfriend. Do we have a copy of that photo on file?"

I flipped through the papers. "No photo." I fingered another report and skimmed the contents. "After they interviewed Lorne Tugg, investigators dismissed Kim Barley. They suggested she was a woman who had felt rejected by him. In other words, they wrote off the case as a woman's spite based on jealousy."

"We'll get the story straight when we visit her this morning. I just called her to set up a meeting."

Something else niggled at me. "What about the storage site the investigators visited? The one Lorne Tugg had leased. I saw a report on that somewhere." I leafed through the file. "Here it is. It states that the owner noticed a foul smell coming from the storage site that Lorne Tugg had leased. When he asked him about it, Lorne explained that he had gone hunting, gutted the animal, and promised to clean up the mess with bleach later." I winced. "How gross!"

"You'd think that a hunter would have handed the animal over to a slaughterhouse, right?"

I refused to give it another thought. "Investigators reported that Lorne vacated the premises months before his lease expired. The new lessee of the storage site also complained about a weird smell, so the owner hired professional cleaners. They identified the stench as suspicious."

"The owner called the police," Ryan said. "They arrived with a cadaver dog and confirmed a corpse residue scent. Investigators found fingerprints on the outer door of the storage unit, but there was no match in the police database. No trace of Vicky's DNA there either."

I read the last line of the report. "Investigators suspect that Lorne Tugg was a fake name."

"It's possible. I checked the usual databases recently and found no criminal records under that name."

"If he's using a fake name, he must be hiding something."

"He's probably used several aliases by now. Like I said, he's disappeared into thin air."

I closed the file. "Which of the two witnesses do we interview first? Kim Barley or the storage owner?"

"Kim Barley." Ryan gulped down the rest of his coffee. "The storage owner definitely merits a visit afterward. We'll go through the same routine as previous investigators did. The smallest thing might pop up that these witnesses originally forgot to mention to police. If we're lucky, we'll pick up on crucial evidence they didn't realize they had."

I was counting on it.

11

———————

The storm had passed by the time we drove out to our destination, but the sluggish traffic on main roads persisted. It wasn't a problem for Ryan. He knew all the shortcuts. After we parked on the street, Kim Barley buzzed us into the apartment building.

I followed Ryan through the double doors. Compared with the grimy lobbies of similar structures in the area, this lobby was the cleanest I'd seen so far. A floral scent permeated the air, adding to the freshness.

Lorne Tugg, the third suspect in the Vicky Johnson kidnapping case, had lived in the same apartment building as Kim decades ago. That Kim still resided here after all these years and agreed to meet with us was promising.

The middle-aged woman with long auburn hair smiled warmly as she welcomed Ryan and me into her second-floor apartment. "Can I offer you coffee? Water?"

"No, thanks," Ryan replied for both of us as we sat down on the paisley couch. "We won't be here long."

Kim settled across from us on a matching love seat. "You mentioned on the phone that you're investigating a cold case."

Ryan retrieved his phone and accessed his notes. "That's right. I'd like to ask you a few questions about someone you might know. Lorne Tugg."

Her hand flew to her throat. "Oh my goodness! I haven't heard that name in ages."

"How do you know him?"

"He lived in this building for a while."

"Would you have a photo of him?"

"No, I don't."

"Can you describe him?"

Kim paused, remembering. "He was of average height and muscular. He worked out in a gym every day, or so he told me. He had a quiet nature about him when we were alone. Almost calming."

Ryan took notes. "What about his behavior around other people, like friends or neighbors?"

"I didn't get to meet any of his friends. All I can say is that he was an energetic, friendly man who talked to everyone. He loved kids and handed out candy to them on Halloween. That's how I met him. I had taken my little ones trick-or-treating in the building."

"What did Lorne do for a living?"

"He worked for delivery companies on a contract basis."

"What companies?"

"I don't know. He never mentioned them."

I raised another topic. "Kim, police records imply you had a close relationship with Lorne."

Kim gently pushed a strand of hair away from her face. "I wouldn't say it was a *close* relationship. I invited him over for dinner a few times. Most men ran the other way when I mentioned I had young kids, but Lorne hit it off with them from the start. He bought them toys, books, and candy. He'd sit them on his lap and read stories to them after dinner."

My heart pumped faster. "What kind of stories?"

"Children's stories. You know, fairy tales." She smiled at the memory. "The kids flipped through the books so often that the pages got ratty."

"How old were your kids at the time?"

"Joshua was five and Sarah was four."

"Did you ever leave them alone with Lorne?"

Kim jerked upright. "Oh, heavens, no."

"Why not?" I asked.

"Long story." She stopped, then noticed I was waiting for her to continue. "I admit I was infatuated by Lorne's good looks, his polite manner, the way he loved to be with my kids... You know, all the stuff that counts in a serious relationship. I finally got the courage to ask him out on a real date. Just the two of us. He refused."

"Did he say why?"

"He didn't have to put it in words. He showed me a photo of his blonde girlfriend and him in Mount Royal Park. He had his arm around her. They were smiling." She shrugged. "Hey, I'm no fool. I got the message."

"What happened afterward?"

"I ended it," Kim said. "I told Lorne I didn't want to see him anymore and to stop calling me. He'd knock at my door anyway and always with gifts for the kids. Naturally, they enjoyed his company. Even after I told him to stop coming over, he'd still pop in. That's when he started to give me the creeps." She crossed her arms in a protective gesture. "I reported him to the police and told them he was harassing me. To be honest, I didn't want him anywhere near my kids."

Though the police report had noted Kim's complaint, I needed to hear what happened next straight from her. "What did the police do about it?"

"Nothing. A week later, a neighbor told me Lorne had moved out. Honestly, if he hadn't left, I would have."

Ryan asked her, "Are you certain you have no pictures of Lorne?"

"I'm sure," Kim said. "He didn't like having his picture

taken. I found that strange. After all, someone else had taken a picture of him with his girlfriend."

"Would you be willing to work with a sketch artist?"

Her eyes widened. "A sketch artist? Is Lorne wanted by the police?"

"He's a person of interest."

"Oh my goodness!" She put a hand to her chest. "Does it have anything to do with the case you mentioned?"

"We'd like to speak with him," Ryan said, dodging the question.

Kim hesitated. "Well, I don't know if I can describe him. I mean, it's been twenty years. My memory isn't what it used to be. I don't think I can..." She babbled on.

Her fear was so palpable that it sent chills up and down my spine. It also sparked a memory about something she said earlier. "Kim, did you keep some of the things Lorne gave your children?"

She relaxed a little, as if I'd given her a way out of a difficult situation. "Yes. A couple of souvenirs. Every mother does. Why?"

"Can we see them?"

"Sure." She went into another room and soon returned holding a snow globe and a children's book. "My kids fought over this Cinderella book one day. They ripped a few pages and Lorne taped them up. Sarah was fond of fairy tales, especially this one, so I kept it."

Ryan pulled out a pair of vinyl gloves and slipped them on. "Is it okay if we hang onto these items for a while?"

"Of course." Kim handed them to him. "Can you tell me why you want them?"

He slid an evidence bag out of his pocket, then carefully placed the two objects inside it. "I'm sorry. I can't discuss that."

A pained expression crossed Kim's face, implying that she understood what was happening. "This is really serious, isn't it? Where is Lorne Tugg now?"

"We don't know," Ryan said.

I returned to a previous topic. "We realize you might be troubled by our request, Kim. Please understand that it would really help us if you could meet with our sketch artist."

She chewed her lips. "I'm sorry. I can't do it. I babysit my grandchildren almost every day. If the police don't know where Lorne Tugg is, and you're collecting evidence for a reason you won't share, I don't want to take the risk of identifying him. What if he comes after me?"

As we walked back to the car, Ryan said, "Kim is the only person who might be able describe Lorne Tugg in detail. Too bad we couldn't convince her to sit with the sketch artist."

"I don't blame her," I said. "She's petrified that he'll find out."

"It happens a lot. Fear prevents witnesses from stepping forward. They later offer the police a piece of information that could have helped to solve a case years earlier."

I opened the passenger door. "You never know. She might change her mind."

Ryan slid in behind the steering wheel. "I didn't want you to have a disturbing experience in front of Kim, so I held onto these until now." He handed me the bagged items.

I touched the snow globe through the evidence bag. How appropriate. Another symbol of childhood innocence.

I waited but nothing promising emerged. "I sense strong anticipation. Nothing else."

"It could be Kim's feelings about Lorne," Ryan suggested. "She was the last person to hold the snow globe."

"It doesn't work like that." I tried again. "Sorry, I'm not getting anything else. I'll try the book."

Cinderella. Coincidence? Not really. Every little girl loves Cinderella. And Kim did say it was her daughter's favorite book.

As with the snow globe, I sensed excitement but nothing more. My confidence was waning. Why wasn't I able to get any insights?

"Sorry," I said. "Nothing from the book either. Just more anticipation." I didn't want to catch the disappointment in his eyes, so I stared out the front windshield.

Ryan started the engine and didn't try to hide the frustration in his voice. "Forget it. We'll get a fingerprint analysis from the tape in the book. Forensics does incredible work these days."

I mumbled something in agreement. Defending myself was useless. He might take me for a worse loser than I already was.

As I repositioned the evidence bag in my lap, I noticed a tiny yellow sticker on the base of the snow globe. "Hey, I didn't see this before." I held up the snow globe so that Ryan could see the sticker.

"What's printed on it?"

"Bitsy Toys. It could be the name of the shop." I hastily pulled out my phone from my handbag and almost dropped it in my eagerness. I tapped a few keys and searched online. "Here it is. It's a Montreal toy shop." I gave him the downtown address.

"What a lucky break!" Enthusiasm energized Ryan's voice. "We have enough time to drive there and back before our next meeting."

∼

Guy Lafontaine looked as if he had owned Bitsy Toys for centuries, not decades. His white beard, a crown of snowy hair, and a portly girth offered a comforting familiarity to parents and children as they rummaged through the busy toy shop. From electronic games to plush animals to arts and crafts, the store was a child's paradise.

Mr. Lafontaine smiled when Ryan showed him the snow

globe inside the evidence bag. "Yes, I've sold lots of those globes over the years. Follow me."

He led us to a shelf where dozens of snow globes in different themes were displayed. There were none like the one Kim's children had received.

"We're asking you to go back twenty years," Ryan said to him. "Do you remember the buyer of this specific snow globe?"

As Mr. Lafontaine peered at it again, his bushy eyebrows arched in surprise. "Yes, I do recall selling a dozen of this model to a man who bought the same number of fairy-tale books. If it hadn't been for the large quantities, I wouldn't have remembered him."

"Can you describe him?"

"His appearance escapes me, as do so many things these days." He let out a hearty laugh, then raised a forefinger. "Except for one thing. He paid in cash."

"Did he say why he bought the items?" I asked him.

"No, and I didn't pry," Mr. Lafontaine said. "He could have been a schoolteacher. They hand out little gifts to their students on occasion, like rewards for doing well in class."

My instincts about the mysterious snow globe customer followed a different path. I suspected that Lorne Tugg had plotted to carry out his devious goals by lavishing young kids with these simple gifts. If I was right, Kim Barley might have narrowly escaped losing her children to a potential pedophile.

What bothered me to no end was that I couldn't get a reading of Lorne Tugg or anyone else when I held the snow globe and fairy-tale book. Aunt Elaine had often told me that my ability would increase over time, not diminish. So what was wrong with me?

Another questioned remained: Did the anticipation that I perceived from the objects come from the children?

Or did it come from Lorne Tugg himself?

12

Jim Cott, the landlord of the storage unit that Lorne Tugg had leased twenty years earlier, was a short, stout man with a loud voice and a jovial manner. We doubted that he could describe his former tenant, let alone recall him by name.

"You bet I remember the name," Mr. Cott said, surprising Ryan and me. "How can anyone forget a renter who paid the last three months before his lease was up? Others had skipped town without paying, so it sure helped to make up for the loss." He chuckled.

A reflection from the gigantic chandelier hanging in the foyer of Mr. Cott's home bounced off the floor tiles. To the left was a living room with a full bar and cozy sofas, not to be outdone by a games room equipped with a pool table on the opposite side of the foyer. I imagined that the other rooms in the sprawling ranch-style bungalow were furnished in similar style. Contrary to the man's complaints about nonpaying tenants, his rental property investments were apparently successful.

"Can you describe Lorne Tugg?" Ryan asked him.

Mr. Cott shook his head. "Sorry, can't help you there. I've seen hundreds of customers come and go over the years."

Ryan scanned the notes on his phone. "Did he say why he was leaving before his lease was up?"

"I think it had something to do with his mother..." Mr. Cott scratched the back of his head. "Oh, yes. She had passed away. He had to leave town to settle things."

"Did he mention the name of the town?"

"No."

"Did he leave a forwarding address?"

"No."

Ryan glanced at his notes. "What kind of vehicle did he drive?"

"A white cargo van," Mr. Cott said. "I remember because it was filthy when he came by to lease the unit. I forget the make, though."

"Do you know what he did for a living?"

"I believe he worked in delivery."

"Who was his employer?"

"No idea."

I joined the conversation. "Mr. Cott, there was a complaint about a foul smell after Lorne Tugg vacated the premises. Police used a cadaver dog to confirm a dead corpse residue scent in the storage unit. Do you remember that?"

He grimaced. "Jeez! How can I forget?"

"Can you tell us what happened?"

"When I noticed the smell, I called Lorne Tugg to ask him about it. He told me he'd gone hunting and had cleaned out some animal. I believed him. I mean, what do I know about hunting? I'm a city guy." He grinned.

"What did he say?"

"He promised he'd wash the place out with bleach."

"Did he?"

"Yes. I leased the storage unit to another customer months after he left, but he complained about a lingering stench."

Mr. Cott's replies matched our investigative records so far.

"What did you do?" I asked him.

"I was forced to cancel the lease and hire a professional cleaning company. The cleaners almost gave me a heart attack when they said a corpse might be the cause of the stench. They didn't have to tell me twice. I called the police right away. They sent over a forensics team. They went through the place from top to bottom. If they found something important, they were tight-lipped about it."

"Is that storage unit currently available?" Ryan asked.

"Let me check." Mr. Cott pulled out his phone and tapped several keys. "Yes, it is."

"Do you mind if we check it out?"

Mr. Cott gaped at him. "What for? There's nothing in there."

"We would like to see it..." Ryan hesitated. "For record purposes."

"Now?"

"Yes."

On the drive to Mr. Cott's storage facilities, he told us the units were rented on a short-term basis, usually monthly. "In Lorne Tugg's case, I think it was a six-month lease. And before you ask me, I rarely saw him on the premises. I supposed he worked during the day and came by at night." He pointed ahead. "Pull up to the next one."

As soon as Mr. Cott raised the roll-up door to the storage unit, Ryan stepped inside. He strolled around, inspecting the walls and corners. At one point, he stopped and gazed up at spots of mold in a corner.

I caught on. He was putting on a performance for me. Our time was limited, so I quickly followed him inside.

Sudden pain shot through my legs, and extreme fear took hold of me. I felt faint and leaned against the wall, willing the throbbing and the spinning to stop.

"Miss, are you okay?" Mr. Cott asked me.

The perceptions kept coming. More pain. Blood spurting everywhere.

I was vaguely aware of Ryan wrapping his arm around my waist. "You need fresh air." He led me outside.

The aching and dizziness subsided. I took a deep breath and slipped a hand inside my pocket to clutch the crystal. "I'm okay now."

Ryan let go of me, yet his troubled look told me he wasn't convinced I was okay.

"Sorry, my allergies are acting up." I smiled at both men.

"Yeah, it can get a little moldy in these units sometimes," Mr. Cott said, unintentionally supporting my excuse. "I keep meaning to get this unit cleaned again. Since there are other units available, I've been putting it off."

Ryan asked him, "Is there anything more about Lorne Tugg that you can tell us?"

"You tell me first, Sergeant. Is Lorne Tugg wanted for a criminal offense? The last thing I need is trouble knocking at my door."

"He's a person of interest."

Mr. Cott swallowed hard. "Believe me, I'd like to help the police, but I don't know much about him. All I can tell you is that he paid the rent on time. I wish all my tenants were like that. Apart from the stench he left behind, I didn't have a problem with him. And I'm not asking for any in the future."

After we drove Mr. Cott back home, Ryan lost no time. "What the hell happened back there, Amber? Spare no details."

His sudden interest intrigued me, as did the furrow along his brow. Was he curious about my insights, or was he concerned about my well-being?

I stuck with a realistic answer. "I felt pain in my legs. It was a sharp pain, like someone had cut me with a knife. I thought I was going to pass out."

"I thought so too. You got real pale." He stole a glance at me. "Did you learn anything else?"

I told him what I'd experienced. "A living creature died in there. It was brutal, but I don't know if it was a person or an animal."

"What about Lorne Tugg? Anything on him?"

"No. Nothing on any of the people who might have leased the unit. You need to understand that I can't control what comes to me."

Ryan steered the car around a corner and said nothing, allowing self-doubts about my capabilities to fill the silence.

I needed to redeem myself, even if I put my credibility on the line. "I didn't have a chance to tell you what I sensed when I held Vicky's second slipper, the one the Johnsons found on their porch." I briefed him about the cold, dark place I'd experienced and suggested it might be a pine box or other rigid structure.

"It doesn't change anything," he said. "After all these years, Vicky's death is the most probable outcome. Whether or not we find her remains is another matter."

So much for boosting my credibility.

The launch of Vicky Johnson's page on the police website produced an unexpected call to the Info-Crime line. After Nadia gave us the details, Ryan and I headed out to interview the new witness.

Mrs. Barbara Bishop lived in a bungalow five streets over from the Johnsons. Framed photos of her children and grandchildren dotted a wall in her living room next to a bay window that looked out onto Morton Park.

After she welcomed us in, Ryan began the conversation. "Mrs. Bishop, you called the Info-Crime line to report you'd seen suspicious activity the night Vicky Johnson went missing."

"Well, I'm not sure if what I saw is related to the case or not.

I have to confess that it's been bothering me ever since the poor child went missing." Her thin lips twitched.

"We're glad you called us," I said. "Be assured that we'll keep whatever you share with us in strict confidence."

She managed a smile. "Thank you. My husband passed away six months ago. I live alone and worry about my safety."

"Can you tell us what you saw that night?"

"It was all very strange." Mrs. Bishop paused, as if she were recalling the memory. "It was past eleven at night. I'd just finished watching a movie on TV. I felt a headache coming on, so I went to the kitchen to get a pill and a glass of water. I happened to glimpse out the bay window here and saw a white van parked across the street. A man was placing a bundle into the rear of the van."

Ryan entered notes on his phone. "Can you describe the man? What was he wearing?"

"He wore a heavy coat with a hood. I couldn't see his face. It was too dark anyway."

"What size was the bundle? Can you give me any details?"

"I can't say exactly. He was holding it with both arms, like this." Mrs. Bishop extended her arms forward, palms up. "I thought his dog had run away, and he'd wrapped a blanket or sheet around it. A runaway dog was, and still is, a frequent occurrence around here. Every third resident owns a dog. They let their pets run free in the park across the street, so I didn't think twice about it."

"Did you hear the dog bark?"

"No. The windows were closed."

"Then what happened?"

"Nothing much. The man got in the van and drove away."

I asked her, "Did anyone else in your house witness what you saw?"

"No," Mrs. Bishop said. "My husband was asleep at the time. It all happened so fast." She smiled apologetically.

The anonymous tip about George Simon surfaced in my

mind. "Mrs. Bishop, have you ever contacted the police regarding the man and his van before?"

"No. To this day, I didn't say a word to the police or anyone else about it." She wrung her crinkly hands. "After Vicky's disappearance, police investigators canvassed the neighborhood. My husband told them about a video surveillance system in the park across the street. I didn't hear anything more from them."

"What prompted you to call the Info-Crime line today?"

"When Christine Johnson—she and I are old friends—told me that her daughter's second slipper had been left on their porch the other day, I finally decided it was my duty to call the police."

Ryan asked her, "How long have you known the Johnsons?"

"More than twenty years. We moved into this neighborhood at about the same time. I met Christine through a bowling club." She sighed. "I regret I didn't contact the police right after Vicky vanished, but I wasn't feeling well that night and didn't make the connection to the van right away. When I thought about it weeks later, fear took hold of me and I decided to keep it to myself. The possibility has tormented me for decades."

"What possibility?"

Mrs. Bishop grew teary-eyed. "That the man I saw that night could have been the person who kidnapped Vicky."

13

Ryan slid into the driver's seat and buckled up. "Another white van. That's all we need."

"It could have been a coincidence," I said. "A man collecting his stray dog in the park, like Mrs. Bishop said."

"And yet, we can't dismiss the tip on the Info-Crime line about George Simon's white van." He sighed. "Anyway, we'll have to put our theories about the van aside for now. I scheduled another meeting for us in a few minutes."

"Oh? More witnesses?"

"One more. He's the manager of the therapy support group that Tony Bruneau joined."

Although I was curious to find out more about Tony's past, the truth was that he'd recently dug a deeper hole for himself by speaking with youngsters in a schoolyard. What if Ryan was right? If Tony had defied parole conditions, it didn't matter whether he attended the support group meetings or not. He'd be back behind bars in no time.

On a positive note, there was a slight chance that his support group manager might put in a good word for Tony, and he might avoid more jail time. We'd find out soon enough.

~

Inside a low-rise building in the city's north end, we met with Cane Potter, a former wrestler turned manager of therapy sessions for ex-convicts. His six-foot-four frame and muscled torso would deter anyone to even think about breaking the house rules. I couldn't envision scrawny Tony Bruneau testing the limits and inviting Cane's anger.

Cane eased his body into an oversized armchair across his desk from Ryan and me. Hugging the wall behind him were boxes stacked in columns five feet high and identified with alphabetical ranges. "How can I help you?"

Ryan began with a personal question. "How long have you managed therapy groups?"

"Twenty years and counting. I suffered a serious injury that put an end to my wrestling career. When a friend mentioned a job opening at this place, I jumped at the chance."

"What kind of people join these therapy groups?"

"Mostly ex-cons. They come here, try it out for a while. Some leave. Others have stuck around for years. They served their sentence and are working hard at making a new life for themselves."

"Any repeat offenders?"

Cane nodded. "Lots. They come back here because they know it's an okay place where they can socialize. Most other sites are off-limits to ex-cons anyway."

"Is there any anonymity here?" I asked him.

"None needed. They know one another from their time in jail or have mutual acquaintances."

"What if they want anonymity?"

"If an ex-con wants anonymity, he can access online support groups instead."

Ryan asked, "Do any of the ex-cons give you trouble?"

"We've had a few," Cane said. "If we notice deviant behavior, we raise the alarm and alert the authorities. The ones who are asked to leave the group usually don't come back." He leaned back and folded his muscular arms. "Unless they want to deal with me personally." A grin lightened the resolve in his expression.

"What about Tony Bruneau? He told us he was a member here."

"He joined years ago, left, then came back. I'm not sure he'll stick it out this time."

"Why not?"

"He seems to be trying, but I'm not convinced he's serious about reforming. Call it a gut feeling." He placed a hand on his taut stomach.

I sensed that Cane was a no-nonsense type. His attitude and replies suggested he'd have a hard time defending Tony to his parole officer.

Curiosity prompted me to ask him, "Does Tony have any close friends here?"

"Not that I know of. He's a loner. Most of them are."

Ryan dug out his phone and studied his notes. "Does the name Enzo Malta ring a bell?"

"Sure does." Cane leaned forward. "When I started working here, Enzo and Tony hung around together. Not long. A few months or so. Enzo had a lot of contacts. He managed to get a job delivering products for a dairy company. He didn't drop by here as often after."

"Do you know the name of the company he worked for?"

Cane stuck out a thumb toward the piles of boxes behind him. "We're in the process of transferring our old files to an automated database. Give me a sec. I'll check if Enzo's file made it into the system." A quick search on his computer proved successful. "Yes. He worked for Creamy Dairy Company."

Ryan took note of it.

"Hang on. I'll look it up for you online." Moments later, Cane swung the monitor around so we could see the screen.

Creamy Dairy Company's website featured a diverse line of

products from milk to cheese. Its fleet of white cargo vans displayed a modest blue decal of the company name in an upper corner and little else.

Another white van.

I couldn't ignore the probability that Tony had borrowed Enzo's van to kidnap Vicky from her home. Finding proof to support that theory would be a hurdle, though.

Ryan took a photo of the website. "Do you happen to have an employer on record for Tony during that same period?"

"Let me see if Tony is in the system." Cane searched through computer files. "Here it is. Small jobs here and there. Cleaning services, grocery packer... He was collecting social assistance most of the time."

"Getting back to Enzo Malta...did you know he was dead?"

"Yes."

"How did you find out?"

"Tony told me Enzo had to be hospitalized. Next thing I knew, Enzo had died from a drug overdose."

Ryan shared my suspicions on the drive back to work. "Tony could be playing us. Something tells me it wouldn't be the first time." He huffed in annoyance. "This case is turning out to be a web of warped leads. It's no wonder that former investigators had no time to unravel it."

I understood his exasperation but wasn't ready to give up. "We have the name of the dairy company that Enzo worked for. As long as we have a lead to pursue, there's hope."

"Right. I'll set up a meeting with the manager there as soon as I can."

Moments after our arrival at the station, Ryan received a call from forensics. They hadn't succeeded in obtaining more details about the young man in Mr. Caron's home surveillance video. The midnight visitor who had dropped off the missing slipper at the Johnson home remained a mystery.

A dead end.

I accessed Vicky Johnson's website page. There were no viable leads, only spam comments, which I deleted. No more calls to the Info-Crime line either.

In the meantime, Ryan followed up with forensics about the items we'd collected from Kim Barley. They found no matches on the RCMP database for the fingerprints lifted from the snow globe. Results were the same for the fingerprints on the fairy-tale book that Lorne Tugg had bought for Kim's children.

More dead ends.

Contradictions about each of the three suspects in Vicky's abduction case continued to plague me. Were any of our three suspects guilty, or did they seem suspicious because of circumstantial evidence? Unproven theories floated in my mind. Three stuck out:

First, Tony Bruneau could have borrowed Enzo's white van to kidnap Vicky. That Tony hadn't reformed was likely, especially since a teacher had identified him as the man who'd recently stood by the schoolyard fence. She'd seen another man lingering by the school but couldn't describe him. According to Ryan, more than one serial killer frequently lived within the same vicinity. That idea alone turned my blood cold.

Second, George Simon's unconfirmed alibi about visiting his mother in the hospital the night Vicky disappeared was troubling. He told us he'd driven a white van decades ago, which supported the anonymous tip about him to the Info-Crime line. Was Mrs. Bishop's witness statement about a man placing a dog in the rear of his white van beyond coincidental? Could George have kidnapped Vicky and tucked her inside his van instead?

Third, Lorne Tugg—or whatever name he went by these days—was a man of dubious ethics. To complicate matters, he had driven a white cargo van decades back. That I couldn't get a clear sense of his soul bothered me immensely, yet I debated whether he was as feasible a suspect as Tony Bruneau or George Simon. My psychic perceptions of the storage unit would have been easy to accept if I wanted to believe he'd killed Vicky there. Maybe it was true that he'd gone hunting and gutted an animal. It was too late anyway. Police investigators had lost the chance to prove he was connected to Vicky's disappearance long ago.

My investigative job was a far greater challenge than I could have imagined. If I couldn't use my gift to help solve cold cases, what was the purpose? How could I face Uncle Ted after he showed so much confidence in me?

If Ryan and I couldn't even solve one case, the lieutenant would have to close down the department. How would I possibly find my parents' murderer without access to police files and resources?

With mounting pressure to solve Vicky's case, time was running out. I needed answers, and I knew just the person who could help me.

14

The sound of broken glass awakened the little girl from a deep sleep.

A man was shouting in the kitchen downstairs. He sounded so angry.

Two loud gunshots rang out in the darkness.

The little girl jumped out of bed but stopped at her bedroom door. She remembered how her parents had told her to hide in the safe space if she ever heard scary noises in the house.

She rushed into her bedroom closet, closed the door, and scrambled over toys and stuffed animals to the farthest corner. She fumbled in the dark, passing her hands along the back wall until she found it: a bear's wood nose glued to a secret panel. Her father had decorated the panel with a colorful stencil of baby animals to hide the nose. She slid open the panel and crawled into the safe space behind it, then closed the panel and pulled the safety latch.

She waited and listened. All she heard was the sound of her heart beating in her chest.

Soon heavy feet thumped up the stairs and along the hallway. It wasn't her father. He didn't make a lot of noise when he walked.

The man was getting closer.

Her mother screamed.

More shots rang out.

Intense danger overwhelmed the little girl, and she could barely breathe.

The man pounded into her bedroom and flipped the bedcovers over, toppling a table lamp to the floor with a crash. He shouted a word, one that her mother said was on the bad list. His voice was loud and grumpy. He was in a bad mood.

The little girl held her breath. He mustn't find her.

The man slowly moved around, causing the wood floor to creak. "Come out, honey." His voice wasn't as loud now. "I won't hurt you."

The little girl didn't move. She was so scared. She just wanted the man to go away.

But he stomped toward the closet door instead and opened it.

The beam from his flashlight shone through the fine slits around the panel and crept onto her pajamas.

The man stepped over toys and ran his hand along the back wall. He was getting closer to the secret bear knob. And to her safe space!

She drew herself into a tight ball, so tight that her chest hurt.

The man found the bear knob! He grabbed it and struggled to open the panel door.

No! She covered her mouth and held back a scream.

There was a loud crack as the knob broke free in the man's hand, leaving a tiny hole in the panel where the screw used to be. He stepped back, then silence.

He couldn't have left. She hadn't heard his footsteps down the hallway.

The little girl was curious to see what the man looked like. She leaned slightly forward and peeked through the hole.

The night-light in her room cast a faint glow on the man. He was standing and wiping his sweaty face with a gloved hand.

She hastily drew back, hoping that he wouldn't peek through the hole.

She heard the floor creak as he moved in closer. He grunted as he tried to force open the panel door but stopped.

Sirens blared in the distance.

The man shouted more bad words and threw something hard against the panel door before he ran out of the room.

The little girl shook with fear but stayed where she was. Her parents had told her not to leave her hiding place until they came to tell her everything was okay. "Mommy! Daddy!" she wanted to call out but was too afraid. The bad man might come back.

It was so dark in the safe place. And she had to go to the toilet. She hoped her parents would come to get her soon. She closed her eyes and wished very hard.

She heard more steps coming up the stairs.

A female voice called out her name and spoke gently. She sounded kind, like her mother, so the little girl believed her when she said it was safe to come out.

Though the ceiling light was on in her bedroom, black spots danced in her eyes.

The woman wrapped her in a soft blanket from head to foot and carried her downstairs.

The little girl asked for her mommy and daddy. The woman said she needed to take her somewhere else first because her parents were hurt and had to go to the hospital.

To better see what was happening around her, the little girl pulled the blanket from her face. Policemen were moving around in the house. She looked at the woman who was carrying her. She was dressed the same as the policemen and had a nice smile.

As they passed the kitchen, the little girl noticed the bowl of red apples on the counter. A large kitchen knife stood straight up in the bowl. "Who did that? Mommy wanted the apples to make a pie," she said.

The apples suddenly turned into a pool of blood!

⌇

I jerked up in bed, sweat dripping down my face, black spots clouding my vision. I'd experienced the same nightmare often since the night my parents had been murdered. Except this time, it had become much more vivid.

I darted to the bathroom and splashed cold water on my face.

It was okay. I was safe. I was the lucky one who had gotten away.

And I'd have to live with it the rest of my life.

15

———

Nothing had changed in Dr. Laura King's office since I'd visited her six months earlier. Stability was one of the reasons I enjoyed coming here when I needed her advice. Trust was the other reason. Laura was one of the few people who knew about my inherited gift and, like my immediate family, she kept mum about it. For that reason alone, I trusted her implicitly.

Although Laura was in her fifties, age was no barrier between us. She had known my mother for years and had been one of her closest friends. I liked to think of our relationship as a continuity of that friendship. Today I wanted her advice as an accomplished psychologist, historian, and an expert in fairy-tale studies and interpretation.

I settled in the green plush armchair across from her desk. "Thanks for seeing me so early this morning."

Laura studied me over the rim of her eyeglasses. "It's been six months."

I skirted the issue. "I have a new job working with the police." I brought her up to date but held back from telling her that I might lose my job soon if I couldn't solve any of the cases. I didn't want to spoil the moment.

"What about your part-time jobs?"

"I'll only keep the volunteer ones for now."

She removed her eyeglasses and set them on the desk. "Have you had any more recurring dreams lately?"

"Yes, last night."

"Do you want to talk about it?"

"Yes, but in a different context. One that's connected to my job." I took a deep breath. "I want to find my parents' killer, and I need your advice."

Laura steepled her slender fingers, a sign that she was contemplating something else. "Tell me about your dream first. Was it different this time?"

"It was more intense."

"And your feelings?"

I tightened my grasp on the armrests. "I had the same horrible sense of guilt afterward. I can't help it."

She extended her hands in a compassionate gesture. Healing hands, I labeled them. "Amber, we've discussed this many times before. There's nothing you could have done. You were a five-year-old child."

"I can't help feeling guilty."

"It's not your fault your parents forgot to lock the patio door that night after the guests left."

"Yes, it was my fault. A killer crept into our house because he wanted to kidnap *me*!"

"It doesn't define you, your parents, or your values. You were part of a caring family." She leaned against the back of her chair and continued in her usual, unruffled manner. "As we've discussed before, the intruder had stalked your home and others in the neighborhood, waiting for an opportunity to kidnap a child. When the chance opened up to kidnap you, he took it. Sadly, your parents caught him by surprise."

"He killed them! If he'd run off, they'd be alive today. Why did they have to die?"

Laura looked down and calmly arranged several pens next to a notepad. "You already know the answer, Amber. Aside from the fact your parents could identify him, the killer didn't want to compete with them for your attention, so he eliminated them."

"You're right. We've rehashed the topic to death. It doesn't change anything, though. I still think that explanation is ridiculous!"

She shook her head. "Not in *his* mind. He's an insidious manipulator."

"Insidious?"

"He's sneaky and proceeds in scheming ways to claim his victims. He needs to win, no matter what. He doesn't care who gets hurt as he races toward his goal."

"Give him the proper tag, Laura. He's a pedophile. A real sicko! I want to catch him and make him pay for what he did—and is doing—to children."

I was venting and she let me. Because of our long-standing rapport, she often tolerated my livid bursts and repetitious rants about the madness behind my parents' demise. I interpreted it as a freebie therapy session on her part, an outlet on the path to healing. Maybe for both of us.

Laura reached for her prescription pad. "Would you like me to give you something to calm—"

"No," I said, cutting her off. "I refuse to take medication to control the panic attacks. It blocks my thinking and my psychic insights. I need to focus on my work so I can find the killer."

She probed deeper. "Amber, what's the real reason behind your quest?"

I stared at her. "I just told you."

She waited.

"Okay, if you want another reason, here it is. After I was

briefed on investigations into missing children, I concluded it wasn't fair."

"What wasn't fair?"

"That I had escaped a fate they hadn't."

Laura's eyes sparkled with awareness. "How do you feel about that?"

"Guilty! How else? I want to find the kidnappers and save the memory of the children whose lives they stole."

"You're already doing that in other ways, aren't you?"

I gave it some thought. "You mean, like reading to sick kids at the hospital?"

Laura nodded. "It eases the pain of loss when you help those less fortunate, doesn't it?"

"I suppose it does."

She kept her gaze on me and waited.

Yes, I was already helping kids, but the purpose of my visit today was different. This time, I needed answers on a professional level. "I'm sorry. Letting out my frustrations on you won't solve the case I'm working on."

She edged forward. "How can I help?"

"I'm reviewing a twenty-year-old cold case with a fairy-tale connection. I'd like to understand the killer's motive for kidnapping a child."

"Go on," Laura said.

I briefed her on Vicky Johnson's case and the recent appearance of the second slipper on her parents' doorstep. "The police call it the Cinderella case. I wasn't looking for similarities, but the fairy-tale element in my parents' case hit me after I reviewed Vicky's."

"What is the fairy-tale element in your parents' case?"

"There's a photo of a long knife standing upright in a bowl of red apples on the kitchen counter. It was the last thing I saw before the police officer carried me out of the house that night. The photo reminds me of the poisonous apple in 'Snow White' in a twisty sort of way."

"And?"

"Why would the killer stick a knife in the apples? It wasn't the murder weapon. A gun was."

Laura rested against her high-backed chair. "There is much about abductors that professionals don't understand. The workings of an abductor's mind and subsequent actions defy logic in the way that we've come to know. Does that answer your question?"

"Yes. In other words, he's nuts."

She gave me a lopsided smile. "I suppose you might describe it that way in less clinical terms."

"Let me rephrase my question. In my parents' case, could there be a connection to the symbolism of the apple in 'Snow White'?"

She joined her hands. "As you know, I've been working for years on a thesis about the interpretation of fairy tales in today's society. I'd like to keep it a secret until it's published. However, I'm willing to share something with you."

"Sure. My lips are sealed."

Laura continued. "In the fairy tale 'Snow White,' the apple stands for death. The evil queen wants to destroy Snow White with a poisonous apple. In the abductor's mind, it's necessary to bring young children to safety by killing them in order to protect them from worldly corruption."

Her explanation stunned me. "What? That's unbelievable!"

"Not if you see the premise through his way of thinking. The message is that fairy tales create a place of safety. They begin with 'once upon a time,' or 'long ago and far away.' In the abductor's distorted mind, he sees himself as a child protector, a savior of innocent children. Of course, he can't be arrested solely because of his fantasies."

"He kidnaps and murders children! Where's the logic behind his actions?"

"One theory is that the abductor had a ruined childhood. Envy about a 'happily ever after' might be his motive."

"Are you saying that he's jealous of children?"

"That's right," Laura said. "It's also conceivable that he wants to prove life is no fairy tale by going after children based on his notions of specific fairy tales."

"Doesn't that theory contradict what you said earlier?"

"It might sound contradictory. However, the abductor believes that only *he* can promise them a happily-ever-after ending."

It was a lot to digest, and I didn't want to take up much more of Laura's time. I guided the conversation back to the Vicky Johnson case. "How would that promise apply to the Cinderella abduction?"

"The abductor considered the young girl as his little princess," Laura said. "And again, he believed he could give her a happily-ever-after ending."

"Is there a psychological reason behind the teasing of her parents with the second slipper?"

"I wouldn't call it teasing. The abductor wants to enjoy exclusive notoriety. It's all about him. He craves publicity and will do anything to achieve it."

"Publicity? You mean, reveal who he is?"

Laura waved the idea away. "Not in the real sense. Rather, he might expose clues to his personal identity so he can enjoy his place in the spotlight. It's a game that he enjoys playing with law enforcement. A matching of wits, so to speak."

"Why now? Why didn't he reveal himself sooner?"

"It's possible that he's seeking recognition before he gets too old to appreciate it. Or his health is failing. Whatever the reason, he wants to enjoy the publicity before then."

I remembered the video of the mystery man who dropped off the missing slipper at the Johnson home. "Would an abductor ever ask for help? I mean, if he's not in good health, would he trust someone else to help him abduct children?"

"While an abductor might work with other offenders, it's a rare situation. They usually prefer to work alone. However, depending on their age or health, they might require assistance with physical tasks, for example, the disposal of a body."

Her explanation matched Ryan's theory about the mystery man in the video. If he was more than an innocent gofer, we needed to include him as a suspect.

"I doubt it's a coincidence that the two cold cases I'm reviewing have fairy-tale elements," I said. "Do you think the same suspect could be involved in both?"

Laura smiled. "You're asking me to take a wild guess."

"Why not?"

"I could ask you the same thing." She grew serious. "My advice is to use your gift."

"I'm not sure about that. It hasn't helped me very much so far."

"Why not?"

"I have a hard time interpreting my impressions." It was a poor excuse, but I didn't want to get into a psychoanalysis of my mind right now. "Anyway, you're the expert when it comes to fairy tales. Uncle Ted would love to have you on his team." I laughed.

Laura laughed as well. "I'm sure he would. Your aunt, not so much."

It was no secret that she'd dated my uncle before he set his sights on Aunt Elaine. Why Laura never got married, preferring to focus on her career instead, was none of my business. Although she appeared content every time I saw her, I perceived a certain loneliness about her.

"You know, Amber, I'd rather remain anonymous and help you to interpret the criminal evidence as it relates to fairy tales. I don't want to be involved directly with police investigations for the reason I mentioned earlier."

"Your thesis."

"Yes."

Although Ryan had given me pointers about an abductor's psyche, I was interested in Laura's input. "I have one last question. Since the abductor in the Cinderella case is most likely a pedophile, what do I need to know about his personality?"

"Let me begin by saying that pedophilia is a complex disorder," Laura said. "Even though pedophiles are sexually attracted to preteen children, they don't always follow through on their desires. If they do, then they're classified as child molesters. That's the difference."

She basically confirmed what Ryan had already told me.

"As for their personality..." She gazed out the window for a moment. "Contrary to the seedy image one might have of a pedophile, most people would describe him as an all-round nice guy. He could be a company executive, a sports coach, a next-door neighbor, or a cleric. Personalities don't change to suit the crime." She glanced at her watch.

"Your next appointment, right?"

"Yes. In a few minutes."

"I should leave." I stood up. "Thanks for seeing me, Laura."

She rose and came up to me, then hugged me. "As you work through this, Amber, don't forget that darkness fades, but hope remains."

"I'm afraid that my recurring nightmares are dampening my determination. Not to mention my confidence."

The flicker in Laura's eyes told me she believed something else was at the root of my problem. "Things will change once you solve the case. Use your skills as an empath. They won't steer you wrong."

I wasn't so sure.

16

Michael Elliott was a well-known name in Montreal journalism circles. I'd read his articles in *The Gazette* and was familiar with his investigative reporting. His partner, ghostwriter Megan Scott, worked alongside him and added her own sleuthing skills to their efforts. The good-looking, thirtysomething couple had brought more than a handful of criminals to justice, and I couldn't wait to meet with them at the station this morning.

After Ryan had made the introductions, the four of us sat down in the conference room. The table seated ten and had been used mainly for staff meetings involving senior officers. Only now, the lieutenant believed that discussions with outside contributors about investigative cases deserved an equal place at the table.

"As I mentioned in our phone conversation earlier," Michael said to Ryan, "Megan and I are investigating the Vicky Johnson kidnapping. It's part of a new series on cold cases that the newspaper is launching."

I admired Michael's discretion. He could have revealed that the Johnsons had asked for their help, seeing as police investigators had neglected Vicky's case for so long. Instead, he refrained from boasting about it.

"We were happy to find out that your unit was revisiting the same case," Megan said to Ryan and me. "The Cinderella case, I believe you call it."

"That's right," I said. "A call from Vicky's parents when the second slipper showed up is the reason we're taking another look at it."

Ryan shifted in his chair. "Actually, Amber recently joined the investigation, but I've been studying the case for a while. We have no DNA matches or solid leads on the perp so far."

What? Why did he speak about me as if I were a trainee?

"We can pool our resources and help you catch this guy," Michael said, his blue eyes twinkling with interest.

"What have you got?" Ryan asked.

Megan reached for a folder in her portfolio and slid it across the table to Ryan and me. "These are photos of Vicky that the Johnson family gave us. We have their written permission to circulate them freely. You're welcome to use them."

Ryan opened the folder, skimmed through the photos, then passed the file to me.

The pictures of Vicky were taken when she was five years old. In one of them, her young friends gathered around her as she opened her birthday presents. Other family photos were taken at different occasions, like Christmas and on family trips.

I felt a twinge of resentment. The Johnson family hadn't offered Ryan and me these photos when we'd visited them. Then again, why would they?

If Ryan was thinking the same thing, he hid it well. "Thanks," he said. "We'll post them on the public website page we set up for Vicky. Someone might see them and recognize her from years back."

"You can use them on any other social media site that would benefit your investigation," Megan said. "Copies are in the flash drive I've attached to the folder."

"We acquired another item from around the time of Vicky's kidnapping," Michael said. "It's a film clip that shows two suspects entering the police station separately, probably to be interviewed."

Ryan gaped at him. "How did you manage to get your hands on that?"

"I can only tell you that it comes from a reliable source," Michael said. "We always protect the identity of people who provide us with leads."

His demeanor was relaxed. I sensed an honest and truthful person behind his words.

"I understand," Ryan said. "Can we see it?"

"The CD is grainy," Michael said. "I'm using a dependable source who can enhance it free of charge. Do you want a copy of it afterward?"

"Absolutely!" My voice contained more eagerness than I'd planned for.

"That would be great," Ryan said to Michael. "By the way, we have a CD on file in the Cinderella case. It's an old video surveillance clip from a CCTV located in a public space. Can you get that one enhanced too?"

"No problem," Michael said. "We're looking at other cold cases, as you are. There are similarities to Vicky's, yet it's hard to prove that the same guy committed the abductions. Have you considered whether a copycat killer might have been involved?"

"It's a likely theory. Media publicity about the case twenty years ago was readily available to curious copycats."

Megan joined in. "As for the second slipper dropped off at the Johnson family's doorstep, it might be hard to obtain a copy of the original one today. Styles have changed."

"You can find vintage items for sale on numerous online sites," I said. "I saw slippers that were almost like Vicky's."

"Why didn't I think of that?" Megan smiled at me. "So it begs the question: Are we dealing with a copycat or the real perpetrator this time?"

"The second slipper is authentic," Ryan said. "If the real perp dropped it off, he's seeking public attention. He probably wants to brag about how he succeeded in evading the police, especially if he committed the same act multiple times and didn't get caught."

"On the topic of slippers, the Cinderella angle intrigues me," Megan said. "We've seen hints of fairy-tale evidence in other criminal files, haven't we, Michael?" She pushed a wavy strand of auburn hair away from her face as she turned to him.

"Right," Michael said. "It's as if the guy is playing out a fantasy about himself and his young victims. It's so easy for a pro to deceive the innocent."

I recalled what Laura had told me. "He's narcissistic and believes he's the savior of children. It's possible that he kills them to give them a fairy-tale ending."

Ryan threw me a puzzled look. "That's a peculiar theory."

I stood my ground. "It's true. I read an article by an expert on the theory of fairy tales and their relation to child kidnappings." Okay, I'd twisted the facts somewhat to hide Laura's identity, but it was the truth. "An abductor's norms are off the chart, not to mention his way of seeing things. He believes he can save children from a corrupt world."

"His motive sounds feasible to me," Megan said. "He could be living out his fantasies in a way only *he* can interpret them."

"Could be," Michael said. "Question is, is this guy still alive? If he is, how do we get inside his head to find out what makes him tick?"

"From what we've seen in other abduction cases, a predator's behavior can be so unpredictable," Megan said. "What kind of person convinces a child to walk away with him?"

"Someone who has easy access to kids," Ryan said. "Especially if he lives in the same neighborhood as them. It's easier to stalk his prey."

"A guy who can drive around with no questions asked," Michael said. "He might own a vehicle or work as a driver for a company. He's invisible to witnesses, but he has easy access to homes or buildings. No questions asked."

I chimed in. "He's someone who radiates trust. He's sociable and helpful. Your neighborhood nice guy."

"He could be unemployed," Megan said, "and does odd jobs around the neighborhood for extra cash."

Silence hung in the air.

"I guess we have our work cut out for us," Ryan said. His phone rang and he glanced at the screen. "Sorry, I have to take this call." He left the room.

While Michael checked his phone for messages, Megan said, "Amber, from what you said about fairy tales, it sounds like you did a lot of research for the Cinderella case."

"Yes, I did," I said. "The fairy-tale connection intrigued me from the start."

"We did some research too. We obviously didn't find the same sources you did." She smiled, waiting.

I would never betray Laura's confidence, so I moved on. "Ryan and I interviewed the same witnesses and suspects as the original investigators did."

"Any new developments?"

I hesitated. Ryan hadn't mentioned the white van. I wasn't sure why he hadn't. Until I'd have a chance to talk to him, I followed his lead and stayed silent about it. "Nothing solid so far. The challenge is figuring out who's guilty and who's not."

"Tell me about it." Megan rolled her eyes. "That's why I stick to research and let Michael follow his instincts in the field. He's better at it than I am. And much braver!" She laughed.

Michael took his attention off his phone and gave her a warm smile.

There was a deep bond between them that I envied. Maybe one day I would find a man I could trust as much as Megan trusted Michael.

Ryan strolled in and returned to his seat. "Did I miss anything?"

"I have another proposal for you," Michael said, surprising us. "How about creating a video reenactment of the Vicky Johnson kidnapping and running it over the media? The public can call the Info-Crime line with tips. Her kidnapping didn't generate widespread attention back then to the extent we can offer today."

Ryan dithered. "Um... I'll talk it over with the lieutenant and let you know."

"Sounds good," Michael said. "I'll have the enhanced CCTV clip and the unsourced film clip for you soon."

~

I met up with Ryan in the kitchen minutes later. "There are no new comments on Vicky's website page or calls on the Info-Crime line."

"You can't expect a steady flow, Amber. Feedback from the public is unpredictable." He poured coffee into a cup. "I'm hoping that new leads surface from the evidence Michael Elliott promised to hand over."

"Speaking of leads, why didn't you mention our suspicions about the white van to him?"

"Because we don't have solid proof."

That may be true, yet I sensed that he wanted to give himself an advantage in solving the case. "You could have shared that detail. We can use all the help we can get."

Ryan stirred milk in his coffee. "Deep down, Michael is a journalist in search of a banner story. I didn't want him to go chasing after every white van in the area."

"I doubt he'd waste his time doing that. He seemed pretty serious to me."

He shrugged. "Like I said, we don't have any solid proof to offer."

His mind was made up. I deviated to another topic. "Megan said they noticed fairy-tale links in other cold case files they were reviewing. Our three suspects might be linked to more abductions. It wouldn't hurt to skim through other files."

He took a sip of coffee, then placed his cup on the counter. "Vicky Johnson's case has taken all our time so far. We can't do the legwork for more cases right now."

"Then we'd better find a damn new strategy soon," I blurted in anger.

Ryan raised his hands in the air. "Slow down! What's this all about?"

"You want the truth?"

"Yes."

I folded my arms. "You didn't have to make it sound as if I were a trainee. I put my fair share of effort into this investigation, you know."

He drew his eyebrows together, concentrating. "You're taking it the wrong way, Amber. I was trying to show them that we were on top of things, that Vicky's case had our attention long before they came on board."

Recognizing his sincerity, I stopped. My venting wasn't going to get me far anyway. My job would vanish in a second if Ryan thought I was trying to top his efforts. I had to persuade him to join forces with me and speak with the lieutenant.

I changed my focus. "Okay. If we really want to show the lieutenant we're making progress, we should listen to Michael. We need to reach out to the public in a different way and ask for their help with the case. A video reenactment is a terrific solution."

"I would have jumped at the chance, Amber, but we have a limited budget," Ryan said. "Producing a video can run into thousands of dollars. The lieutenant won't go for it."

"If we don't ask, we won't know."

"Right now?"

"Why not?"

He appeared to be running a scene through his mind.

"Okay. Let's discuss the fine points first. We have to make a convincing argument."

After a brainstorming session, we met with the lieutenant. He listened as we updated him on the Cinderella case and our recent discussion with Michael and Megan.

Ryan implied that we were close to cracking the case, and that a new media venue under consideration would definitely do it. The passion he put into his argument was quite a stretch, but I played along.

"Lieutenant, we need to increase our appeal to the public," he said. "We can do that with a video reenactment of Vicky Johnson's abduction. We'll use a narrator to mimic a girl's five-year-old voice to drive home the personal aspect of the abduction. Our efforts are guaranteed to bring in clues that will benefit our investigation."

I joined in. "We can use Kim's snow globe and tattered fairy-tale book in the video. We have photos of Vicky that the Johnson family approved for distribution. They're relevant for the time period she was kidnapped. We can also use photo-progression sketches."

Ryan ended our proposal with a grand finale. "We would broadcast the video nationally and share it on *In Pursuit with John Walsh*. Millions of viewers would see it. We're sure to get feedback about it."

Not hesitating, the lieutenant said, "Get the parents' consent first. Let's get this video done ASAP."

Back at our desks, Ryan smiled and said to me, "We're finally getting somewhere." After he obtained approval from Eric and Christine Johnson, he contacted Michael Elliott to confirm we were on board to produce a video reenactment of Vicky's abduction.

Nadia posted the photos that Michael had given us on Vicky's website. Once the video was ready to go, she'd upload it to the website and selected social media sites.

I eagerly pinned the hardcopy photos of Vicky as a child to

the evidence whiteboard in our quasi office. We were finally getting somewhere, and I was so encouraged.

Then why was the excitement of the moment fading away so fast? What was causing a sudden damper on my happy mood?

I took a moment to review the gist of our meeting with the lieutenant. Although he'd given us his approval, it wasn't enthusiasm that I'd detected behind his rapid consent. It was a last-ditch effort on his part to save our jobs.

17

———

The weekend brought a well-deserved occasion to catch up on sleep. Fueled with renewed energy, I cleaned my apartment, did the laundry, and set out to visit an old friend at a local retirement home. Since my work schedule had been busy the last few days, I hadn't had the time to drop in on Mrs. Brody again.

I knocked on the partially open door to her private room. "Hello, Mrs. Brody."

She greeted me with a smile. "Hello. Come on in, Crystal."

As usual, I let it slide.

"Come see what I made in my therapy class." She picked up a set of ceramic coasters from the table by the window. "Dash" was inscribed on each of them.

"They're lovely, Mrs. Brody." I suspected they were for her son, Dash. "Did you make these for someone special?"

She blinked. "Not that I can recall." She put them back down.

Sadness rolled over me. Her family members and friends must have been so disturbed to notice her memory increasingly slip away over the years.

After we settled in our armchairs, I asked, "What would you like me to read today, Mrs. Brody?"

She reached for a book on the table. "This one." She handed it to me, then adjusted the blanket over her lap. "It's my favorite."

Every book was Mrs. Brody's favorite, though *A Tale of Two Cities* by Charles Dickens happened to be one of my favorites. She'd often requested that I read passages from it. Reading the same pages again didn't bother me as long as it made her happy.

I began. "It was the best of times, it was the worst of times, it was the age of foolishness, it was the epoch of belief..."

I'd read several pages when Mrs. Brody's eyes began to close, and she drifted off to sleep. I placed the book on the table, tucked the blanket around her, and quietly tiptoed out.

As I reached the exit door at the far end of the corridor, a little voice prompted me to glance back over my shoulder.

A man was standing outside Mrs. Brody's door. It was Ryan! He knocked on the door, then entered the room.

Aha! I wasn't mistaken. I'd seen him here the last time I visited Mrs. Brody after all.

Did he know her?

Or was he checking up on me?

I set out early Saturday evening for my housesitting job. Once a month, Mr. and Mrs. Mahoney invited me to take care of Duke, their German shepherd. Since they'd be sleeping over at a Bed and Breakfast and coming back Sunday morning, it wouldn't interfere with my plans to watch a movie with Nicole tomorrow afternoon.

After I fed Duke and ate a scrumptious dinner of seafood pasta that the Mahoneys had left for me, I put Duke on a leash, and we stepped out. I enjoyed walking Duke. The money I made was more than decent, and Duke had been trained to obey simple commands like sit, stay, come, and no. He was loving and lavished dog kisses on me every time I visited.

Aside from a young couple across the street and a man in a white baseball cap ahead of me, the sidewalks were bare. We strolled along, past tall trees and manicured lawns at luxurious two-story houses. It was easy to imagine any one of these homes on the cover of a trendy magazine.

As we reached the end of a long residential block that gave way to a park, Duke tugged at the leash, pulling me forward. Bordered by dense trees and shrubbery, the park was deserted, and the landscape lighting was dim.

The place gave me the creeps. "Forget it, Duke. It's dark. Let's go back home."

Duke stared at a clump of bushes and growled. I figured a squirrel had caught his attention, but then he barked and lunged, yanking me forward.

It took all my strength and both hands on the leash to restrain the German shepherd, who weighed almost as much as I did. "No! Sit."

While Duke sat, his focus remained on his original target.

A brisk movement behind the bushes triggered another round of barking. A man wearing a white baseball cap shot up and ran off in the opposite direction!

Duke charged forward.

My arms jerked from the sudden movement, but I held a firm grasp on the leash. "Stay, Duke! Stay!"

The dog obeyed and reduced his barking to a whimper of displeasure.

I hadn't seen the man's face because of the shadows, though that white baseball cap wasn't a coincidence. He was the same man I'd seen earlier. Was he stalking me?

My heart beat faster. "Let's get out of here, Duke."

Unable to shake the sensation that someone was watching me, I raced back to the Mahoney residence, with Duke gratified to keep up with me. Relief flooded over me after I unlocked the front door, rushed inside, and bolted the double locks.

❡

A clattering noise, then a bang against the front door propelled me to my feet. Confused and trying to recall where I was, I realized I'd fallen asleep on the couch at the Mahoneys.

It couldn't be the couple returning from their trip. They weren't due back till tomorrow. Someone was trying to break in!

Duke growled but otherwise stayed motionless on the floor by me.

I looked around for an object I could defend myself with. Not that expensive ceramic vase. No, that priceless glass sculpture wouldn't do either.

The front door swung open and I froze.

Mr. Mahoney supported his wife as she limped into the foyer on a bandaged foot. "Hi, Amber," he said.

I was astounded. "What happened?"

"We went out for a late-night walk in the country with friends. My wife sprained her ankle when she stepped on a rock."

"I was clumsy," Mrs. Mahoney said, wincing in pain. "I looked up when I should have been looking down. I should have known better." She groaned and hung onto the staircase railing.

"Do you need any help?" I asked.

"No, thanks, Amber," Mr. Mahoney said. "We can manage. It's two in the morning. If you don't want to drive back home, you're welcome to stay the night."

"No, it's okay. I'll drive home."

He paid me in cash, adding a little extra like he always did. "Drive safely." He waited until I got behind the wheel, then he shut the front door.

Laden with a container of chocolate ice cream and a bag of potato chips, Nicole arrived at my apartment Sunday afternoon. "It was my turn, so I brought a choice of sweet and salty." She set the ice cream and chips on the kitchen counter. "You don't know how eager I was for today. This week has been a roller coaster of crazy events." Her French accent dramatized her bubbly mood.

"You want to start with the ice cream?" I asked.

"Whatever you want. We'll end up eating everything anyway." She giggled.

I took out two bowls from the cupboard and filled them with ice cream. "Let's go sit down, and you can tell me all about your week."

Sitting on the sofa next to me, Nicole ranted about a busy work schedule, how she had to tend to a disruptive student who came from a broken family, and how she reported a grade-three student who had initiated a bullying incident.

"Talk about responsibilities," I said. "You definitely needed a break."

"There are days when all I want to do is go home and sleep. The next day, I'm happy to go back to the classroom. I love those kids. You know that I do."

"Of course."

Silence fell between us. It was an odd occurrence since Nicole rarely ran out of things to talk about. I sensed uneasiness emanating from her.

She ate a spoonful of ice cream. "I have a question. Remember how I told you about the strange man who stood by the fence and watched the children at recess last week?"

"Yes." My blood turned as cold as the ice cream bowl. "Did he come back?"

"No, but I worry about my first-grade students, especially at recess when they play in the schoolyard. I can't watch each one of them at every moment. We warn the children not to talk to people they don't know. Some of them don't listen. I'm afraid that a child will walk away with a stranger one day. It's so scary. What more can I do?"

"The next time you see a suspicious man by the schoolyard, take note of his features, the clothes he's wearing...you know. Then ask your principal to contact the police."

Nicole scooped more ice cream. "I could take a photo of the man."

"Even better."

"Thanks. Now it's your turn, Amber. Tell me about your new job."

If I revealed that Ryan and I had interviewed witnesses and potential pedophiles, it would overwhelm her, besides being against work policy. Instead I said, "There isn't much to tell. I work with a partner named Ryan. He's about five years older than me."

Nicole's hazel eyes sparkled with curiosity. "Tell me more about him. Is he sexy?"

I would have considered the question intrusive had anyone else asked it. Since it came from Nicole, who enjoyed playing matchmaker, it was typical. "He's okay."

"Just okay? That's it? Describe him."

"He's tall and muscular and looks as if he hasn't shaved in two days."

"Sound sexy to me." She laughed. "Is he married?"

"Not that I know of."

"Why not? You don't talk to each other?"

"We've been busy," I said, trying to change the topic.

Nicole smiled in a teasing way. "Do you like him?"

"It's not like that between us. Ours is a business relationship."

"Uh-huh. That's what they all say." She laughed and ate more ice cream.

Who was I kidding? Ryan's magnetism intrigued me as

much as his evasiveness. Come to think of it, I didn't know much about the man except for his work habits.

It was time to change that. I needed to find out more about him, including why he was sneaking around Mrs. Brody's room right after I'd visited with her.

18

———————

As soon as I arrived at the station Monday morning, I planned to confront Ryan and tell him I'd seen him at the retirement home. Instead, he diverted my attention to the case we were investigating and whizzed me off to our first appointment, briefing me along the way.

Manager Pietro Perri squinted behind bifocals as he studied his computer screen. He'd spent the last ten minutes searching the personnel database of Creamy Dairy Company. "Yes, we did have an employee named Enzo Malta about twenty years ago." He glanced at us from across his desk.

Next to me, Ryan leaned forward in his chair. "How long did he work for you?"

"Several months. He worked in delivery."

"How was his performance on the job?"

"That's confidential information."

Ryan straightened up. "The man is dead. I doubt he would mind."

Mr. Perri returned his attention to the screen and clicked his mouse to open up another window. "His conduct was...uh...questionable, I'd say."

"How?"

"He was fired."

"Why?"

Mr. Perri adjusted his eyeglasses. "Our inspector examined the company van he drove and found heroin. We have a zero tolerance for drug use on the job."

~

Ryan steered the car off Creamy Dairy's rambling premises where a fleet of the company's white delivery vans were parked. "My radar is up about Tony Bruneau and his past connection to Enzo. Who's to say Enzo didn't lend him his van?"

"You mean, to sell drugs? Or to kidnap little girls?" My tone sounded more sarcastic than I intended.

He pressed his lips together. "Look, Amber, I get it. We don't have much to go on except Tony's unproven alibi the night Vicky Johnson disappeared. As far-fetched as it sounds, a connection to Enzo's van could end up being a worthwhile lead."

"Sorry, I didn't mean to come across as skeptical. Since we haven't eliminated the other two suspects yet, I'm trying to keep an open mind."

"It doesn't change anything. Tony could have lied by omission. We'll interview him again and ask him about Enzo's van this time."

The minutes remaining on our drive back to work gave me the chance to ask a critical question. "Why have you been tailing me?"

Ryan scowled. "Tailing you? What are you talking about?"

"I saw you at the retirement home the other day."

"The retirement home?"

"Yes. I saw you there twice."

Surprise drained the color from his face. "I could ask you the same question."

"I have a volunteer job reading to seniors, and I regularly drop in on Mrs. Brody. I saw you walk into her room."

"I wasn't following you." Ryan cleared his throat. "Mrs. Brody is my mother."

I stared at him. "Your mother? Her family name isn't the same as yours."

"She used her maiden name when she moved to the retirement home. It simplified the paperwork."

"Oh." I didn't know what to say. "She's one of my favorite people there."

"I'll keep that in mind." His reply was blunt, putting an end to an awkward conversation.

Unintentionally, I'd discovered a part of Ryan's life that he'd clearly preferred to keep secret. I understood now why he was so upset when George Simon had played head games with his own mother who also suffered from dementia. I didn't pry any further.

We entered the station to discover that Michael Elliott had personally delivered copies of the old CCTV video and the unsourced video as promised. The journalist had used his software contacts to improve the quality of both items and left us a note: *We're pleased with the outcome of the recovery process. Couldn't get a trace on the plate but knew you would!*

As Ryan and I watched the CCTV video, we understood Michael's note. Although the black and white clip was somewhat grainy and it was recorded at night, we could easily make out the images. The scene opened with a man in a hooded coat carrying a large object wrapped in a blanket. Something whitish stuck out of his load as he carried it along the sidewalk.

"Is that a shoe?" I asked Ryan.

He paused the video and peered at the screen. "It could be a child's shoe. Let's watch the rest."

As the video played out, the man carefully placed the bundle in the back of a white van and briefly leaned in. He shut the back doors and got in the driver's seat. The license plate on the rear of the van was clearly visible.

"Talk about a fluky break!" Ryan copied the license number, then called to request an immediate verification.

"It could be what Mrs. Bishop saw through her front window that night," I said.

"But from a different angle. This clip was taken from Morton Park across the street. Former investigators took Mr. Bishop's advice and obtained the CCTV video. I guess they had no time or money to follow through on it."

The final seconds of the video showed the van driving off.

"It's interesting how a white van keeps popping up in our investigations," I said.

"It doesn't help that it was one of the most popular colors among buyers for decades," Ryan said.

"Too bad the man's face wasn't visible. His heavy coat also makes it difficult to estimate his size."

"Technology can only do so much. At least we have the license plate." His phone rang and he answered. Shock registered on his face as he listened. "Okay, thanks." He ended the call, then said to me, "The van was registered to a sole ownership that went out of business years ago. The owner was George Simon."

"What? Does this mean George lied to us? That he could have kidnapped Vicky?"

"We'll find out soon enough. Let's watch the next video first."

Michael Elliott's unsourced video revealed George Simon entering the police station. An unidentified man in a coat with a hood appeared in the next scene. According to the timestamp, each man entered and left the police station within half an hour of each other.

"I couldn't see the second man's face," I said. "I don't think it was Tony. The man is taller and heavier than Tony, although the thick coat can be deceiving."

"He could be a witness that investigators interviewed at the time. Unless these two men were considered suspects, the police might not have videotaped the meetings. I'll ask for a check of police records anyway." Ryan tapped a note on his phone. "Okay. Let's go pay George Simon a surprise visit."

"What about Tony? Weren't we supposed to go to his place to ask about his friend Enzo?"

"He's next."

19

George frantically waved his arms in the air. "I already told you. I visited my mother in the hospital that night."

"You left out a few details," Ryan pointed out as we stood in the hallway of George's apartment.

"Like what?"

"What were you doing in the vicinity of Morton Park late that night?"

George's jaw dropped. "You're not trying to incriminate me again, are you?"

Ryan raised his voice. "Answer the question."

"Georgie, is everything alright?" his mother called out from the living room. She was sitting by the window like the last time we'd visited.

"Everything's fine, Mom," George replied, then spoke to us in a quiet voice. "Let's all sit down. I'll explain everything." He led the way to the kitchen. "Let me clear the table before you sit down." He took away the breakfast plates and rinsed them in the sink, a sign that he was buying time.

While Ryan and I sat waiting, I wondered how George would squirm his way out of this one. He couldn't prove he was at the hospital with his mother when the video showed otherwise.

George soon joined us at the table. "After Dad died decades ago, Mom couldn't afford to live alone. We agreed to combine our resources and share the same apartment. With me working almost every day, Mom was lonely. So I got her a dog. Her name was Boots. Long story short, while Mom was in the hospital for her surgery, a neighbor took care of the dog. Somehow Boots got outside. I drove around late that night and found her wandering near Morton Park. She had an injured paw. I wrapped her in a blanket and set her in the back of my van. That's the whole story."

He sounded very convincing. Either he was an excellent liar, or my internal lie detector wasn't up to par.

"What kind of dog was she?" Ryan asked him.

"A black and white Border Collie. The cutest thing. She had white paws."

White paws? Was that what Ryan and I had noticed in the Morton Park video?

Ryan went on, not indicating whether he'd made the connection or not. "Does the neighbor live around here?"

George shook his head. "He died years ago. So much for proving my alibi."

Ryan found another way to test the man's veracity. "Your neighbor told us you weren't babysitting her kid anymore."

"It didn't work out," George calmly admitted. "I'm okay with that. I've got my hands full taking care of Mom."

Ryan stood up. "Okay, we're done here."

I glanced at George's mother and couldn't explain why I was compelled to go over. "Wait. I'd like to say hi to George's mother." I approached the tiny woman in the oversized armchair. Her feet in white running shoes dangled in the air. "Hello."

She looked up from an old photo album she was leafing through and smiled. "Hello, dear. It's so nice to meet friends of Georgie." She turned away and focused on the photos.

On the windowsill was the same pile of fairy-tale books I'd seen on our last trip here. For reasons unknown, the photo album had won out today.

Mrs. Simon pointed to a picture. "This was taken on my wedding day." Her eyes glistened. "I was so happy then."

I smiled. "It's a lovely photo."

Her loneliness crept under my skin. The album was a connection to her past and, sadly, the only way to keep her memories from completely fading away.

I had a sudden urge to sit with her as she turned the pages. Like other feelings I'd experienced, I couldn't explain it. I slowly walked away.

~

If George was telling the truth, he'd given us a sound reason to support his appearance in the CCTV video from Morton Park. I put my theory to the test as we drove back to the station. "Ryan, I'm not trying to defend George, but he could be telling us the truth about tracking down his dog that night."

Ryan wasn't convinced. "Don't forget that the video clip was black and white, so what we saw could have been a light-pink slipper like Vicky's."

"How can we prove what it was, one way or the other?"

He ignored my question. "It's important to consider the elements in the video. To begin with, the timing fits. George could have visited his mother at the hospital, then kidnapped Vicky later that night."

"Except we can't prove who or what George was carrying in that video. It could have been his dog."

"Or he could be lying through his teeth."

The lapse of decades had given George a convenient way out. While the video raised our suspicions, there was a lack of hard evidence against him. Yet a lingering doubt that he could have been responsible for Vicky's abduction continued to hold our minds hostage.

Would we ever find out whether or not George had lied to us?

~

On our return to the station, Ryan retreated to his desk. He hadn't forgotten about Tony Bruneau. He needed to go over his schedule before heading back out to question him about his friend's company van.

In the meantime, I sat at my desk and checked the Info-Crime line. No messages.

I was about to get a cup of coffee in the kitchen when a call came in. Rather than letting it go to the message center, I answered.

Using a voice changer app, the caller said, "I have information about the abductor in the Vicky Johnson case. I know where he took her."

My pulse quickened. I was glad to be sitting. "Where?"

"It's a place where trespassers aren't welcome. Larkland Park. It's out of town." He provided the coordinates.

Trembling, I scribbled "caller" on a notepad. "How do you know this?"

"He bragged to me about how he'd kidnapped the little girl decades ago and what he did to her."

My stomach did flip-flops. I swiftly fingered the crystal in my pocket. Gaining a measure of composure, I stood up and flapped my notepad at Ryan, who instantly hurried over.

The caller interpreted my silence as hesitation. "Is there a problem? You don't seem interested."

I detected truth behind the camouflaged voice, maybe a man's voice, but pressed him further. "Anyone can call this line and say what you just said. Tell me something more significant."

After a brief silence, the voice droned on. "Her remains are in a pine box. The killer kept one of Vicky's pink slippers as a souvenir. It's like the one the police put on her website."

He had transitioned from using the term *abductor* to *killer*. "Why would he tell you these things? Why *you*?"

"It's a matter of trust."

The line went dead.

I could barely move. The revelation of the pine box confirmed what I'd perceived when I'd held Vicky's second slipper. My insight was not only real, but it was now relevant.

I met Ryan's stare. "You have to hear this."

As he listened to the recorded call, amazement washed over his face. "The pine box. A restricted enclosure. It confirms what you experienced, right?"

"Yes."

"Did you get anything else from the caller?"

"I'm sure it was a man. I sense that he's telling the truth."

Ryan ran a hand over his unshaven chin. "He could be a snitch who has a score to settle. If the killer finds out a revengeful informer contacted us, he'll hunt him down."

Laura's words about the abductor seeking notoriety echoed in my mind. "Maybe not."

"Why would you say that?"

"Maybe the caller *was* the killer."

20

Lieutenant Payton sprang into action right after Ryan and I briefed him about the anonymous call to the Info-Crime line. He coordinated efforts with the Quebec Provincial Police, better known as the QPP, to conduct a search for Vicky Johnson's remains in Larkland Park.

Located in a remote stretch of land north of Montreal, the park was a protected wilderness area managed by the provincial government and closed to the general public. It would be the perfect spot for a killer to sneak in and bury a body.

"With rain in the forecast, the QPP believes that the search could take days or longer," the lieutenant told us. "Let's hope the anonymous caller's tip yields results."

Later that afternoon, a call came in from the parole board. Tony Bruneau's parole officer had knocked at his apartment door on three occasions. There had been no answer. Under a long-term supervision order that Tony had violated on several fronts, the board asked the police for help in locating and arresting him.

Based on what we'd seen during our visit, Ryan requested a

warrant to seize and perform a search of electronic equipment found in Tony's apartment and asked forensics to join us there. "We were going to drop in on Tony sooner or later anyway to talk about his friend Enzo," he said to me. "This development speeds things up."

I couldn't forget the insight I'd had of a bruised and bleeding Tony. "I can't shake the feeling that something bad happened to him. He could be hurt."

"Or maybe he went lurking around in places he shouldn't have." He gave me a pointed look, then slipped into his jacket. "Let's go. Who knows what we'll find."

~

Ryan knocked twice on Tony's apartment door but received no reply. He stepped aside to allow the property owner to use his set of master keys.

I waited in the corridor with the parole officer and a digital forensic examiner while Ryan did a quick search of the ex-con's apartment. After he confirmed if it was safe for us to enter, I followed the others inside.

"Tony's not here," Ryan said to me, stating the obvious. "His puppy is gone too."

"He didn't seem like the dog-walking type to me," I said.

"Yes, but there's nothing like using a cute puppy to lure young children away."

I squirmed at the thought.

The rank stench in the apartment drew my eyes to the dirty dishes strewing the kitchen counter. "I think he left in a hurry," I said to Ryan. "These plates are all yucky like they've been sitting here for days."

After noting Tony's absence and the laptop on the kitchen table, the parole officer said to Ryan, "I'll be leaving now. Please keep me informed if you find anything that further breaches Tony's conditions."

The digital forensic examiner sat down and opened up Tony's laptop. His task was to search for visits that Tony might have made to websites prohibited by the parole board.

"In the meantime, let's take a quick look around," Ryan said to me. "This place might not be a crime scene, but whatever is in here might link Tony to a crime. It could be bloodstains, a receipt, or even a note to himself."

We pulled on our vinyl gloves and walked through a living room littered with empty beer cans, take-out containers, and more dirty plates. I refused to enter the dingy bathroom, though Ryan stole a glimpse inside and frowned.

When we entered Tony's bedroom, I couldn't hide my disgust. "What a mess!"

Clothing, shoes, and other items were scattered around every inch of the room. Did the chaos act as a smokescreen for hiding something?

"There's no trace of his cell phone anywhere," Ryan said. "He must have taken it with him. Are you getting anything?" He placed a finger on his temple.

"Not yet." I picked up a running shoe from the floor. I instantly got an impression of two or more men beating Tony. Fear threw me off balance. I leaned against the wall and slipped a hand into my pocket to clasp the crystal.

Ryan's forehead puckered. "Are you okay?"

"Yes." I described what I'd experienced. "I can't pinpoint the time frame. It could be an event in the past or the future."

"You could be picking up on the mistreatment Tony got in jail from inmates again. That sort of behavior happens more often than we think."

He stirred up a doubt inside me. "Tony did mention how rough it had been in jail for him. Still, the incident was so vivid. As if it happened moments ago."

"You said you didn't know the time frame."

"I know...I meant..." I stammered. "I could feel Tony's fear as if I were there."

Ryan reached for a pair of binoculars on the dresser. "Try this. He probably used them to stalk his prey."

I held them and began to shiver, then hastily placed them on the dresser. "Um... Tony gets very excited when he looks through these."

"I'm not surprised. He's a repeat offender. What we've found here so far makes him a strong suspect in the Cinderella case. And maybe in other cases. He could be our guy."

"Aren't we jumping to conclusions?" I asked, turning his favorite line to my advantage.

The forensic examiner suddenly called out, "Sergeant, I found something!"

As we hurried up to him, Ryan asked, "What have you got?"

The examiner pointed to the screen. "About a thousand photos. Mostly young girls in various stages of undress. Some can't be older than ten years old. Other photos of Tony with kids at summer camp. More photos of kids in schoolyards."

"Seize the laptop and send me an analysis report." Ryan turned to me. "Like I said, these habits are hard to break for some ex-cons."

I grappled to contain the nausea mounting inside me. "Now we know why Tony rushed to close his laptop the last time we were here."

No sooner had the forensic examiner left than Ryan's phone rang. It was Lieutenant Payton. "Yes, Amber is here. I'll put you on speakerphone."

The lieutenant's voice reflected urgency. "We received a report on Lily DeLuca, a seven-year-old girl who went missing from an elementary school this afternoon. We launched an Amber alert province wide in partnership with the RCMP."

Oh, no! Not another child! My thoughts gravitated to the little girl and the worst-case scenarios. What if she'd been sexually assaulted and killed?

The lieutenant continued. "We issued a special press release to the media with the girl's description and other details. I forwarded you a copy."

Ryan's phone pinged but he ignored it.

The lieutenant went on. "My other investigators have their hands full, so I'd like you and Amber to follow up on this case. I spoke briefly with the principal. The girl's parents are on their way to the school. Wrap up your visit as soon as you can, then head out there to interview them."

"Will do."

"Have you located Tony Bruneau?"

"No." Ryan updated him on the photos that forensics had discovered.

"Keep me informed after your visit to the school." The lieutenant ended the call.

Ryan tapped his phone to access the report containing the missing girl's description. He read it out loud. "Lily DeLuca is four feet tall and weighs about fifty pounds. She wears her long brown hair in braids. She was last seen wearing a purple jacket over her school uniform and purple and white running shoes. A witness saw a man with a small dog in the vicinity of the schoolyard shortly before the girl's disappearance. The teacher on supervisory duty claims the girl wandered off the grounds of Blessed Mary Elementary School during afternoon recess."

My stomach felt queasy. "That's where my friend, Nicole, teaches. The elementary school isn't far from here. What if Tony used the puppy to lure the little girl and—"

"My thoughts exactly. Since he didn't get lucky at the other school a block away, he could have extended his stalking radius to three blocks. Blessed Mary school is within that range."

"Tony is on foot. What if he comes back here with the little girl?"

"Then we'd better get the hell out of here!"

Ryan contacted dispatch and requested that police in the area be on the lookout for Tony Bruneau. He wasn't taking any chances. The ex-con was now considered a person of interest in the kidnapping of seven-year-old Lily DeLuca.

21

———

The distress on the principal's face accentuated her wrinkles as she addressed Ryan and me. "To think that one of my young students would walk off with a perfect stranger... It's absolutely horrific." She put a weathered hand over her heart. "I've arranged for Lily's parents to speak with you privately afterward."

"Thank you," Ryan said. "Mrs. Alderwood, are you certain that a stranger lured Lily out of the schoolyard?"

Brown eyes flashed under soft gray bangs. "What other reason is there for a child to wander off like that with no explanation?"

"She could have left with a relative. A trusted friend of the family."

"If that were the case, I'd expect they would have notified the school beforehand. Parents are aware of the rules."

I chimed in. "Children have been known to do unpredictable things. Maybe something unpleasant happened to Lily at school and she left."

The creases in the principal's forehead deepened. "The children know there are rules to follow. They don't leave the grounds during school hours without telling a teacher or supervisor. Isn't that right, Miss Lombardi?" She addressed the young woman sitting in a chair adjacent to her desk.

Her head bent, Miss Lombardi whispered, "Yes, Mrs. Alderwood." Her eyes were red and swollen from crying.

Ryan took up his line of questioning. "Miss Lombardi, we understand that you were the teacher on duty when Lily went missing."

She shifted uncomfortably, further betraying her guilt. "Yes, I was."

"Can you tell us what happened? When did you notice that Lily was no longer in the schoolyard?"

"I was supervising the students outside during afternoon recess," Miss Lombardi began. "One of the students fell and bruised her knee, so I took her inside to get cleaned up. I was only gone a minute or two." Her eyes welled with fresh tears. "When I went back outside, another student told me that Lily had left the schoolyard. I ran to the sidewalk and looked up and down the street, but there was no sign of her. I reported it to Mrs. Alderwood right away."

"Who was the student who came to get you?"

"Gabriella Corti. She's one of Lily's friends."

"Did Gabriella see Lily leave with anyone?"

"I don't know."

I joined the conversation. "We received a witness report about a man with a dog near the school grounds today. Who is this witness?"

"The same student—Gabriella Corti," Miss Lombardi said. "She was quite upset about what happened today. Her parents picked her up and drove her home."

"Can we have the Corti family's contact information?" Ryan asked the principal.

"Of course." Mrs. Alderwood picked up a sheet of paper on her desk and handed it to him. "I had anticipated you'd ask for it."

"Thanks." Ryan folded the sheet and tucked it in his pocket. "Is there anything else either of you can tell us?"

"Not at this time," Mrs. Alderwood said.

"Well...actually," Miss Lombardi began. "I wasn't the only teacher on supervisory duty."

Astonished, Mrs. Alderwood turned to her. "Really? Who else was there with you?"

"Nicole Latour. She teaches the first grade."

My friend Nicole?

My gasp was hidden by the scraping of Mrs. Alderwood's chair against the floor as she rose. "Excuse me," she said. "I'll ask Miss Latour to join us." She walked out.

My cover was blown. I imagined Nicole's reaction when she'd see me sitting next to a detective who was investigating a report about a missing person. I'd never hear the end of it.

Moments later, Mrs. Alderwood and Nicole entered the room. Cutting short the principal's introductions, Nicole gaped at me and said, "Amber!"

Unsmiling, I uttered, "Hello, Nicole."

She stared at Ryan and said, "Hi."

The awkward moment passed when the principal indicated the empty chair next to Miss Lombardi. "Please have a seat, Miss Latour."

Nicole joined her teary-eyed colleague. Her complexion was pale, and she was no doubt concerned about recent events at the school.

Mrs. Alderwood said, "Miss Latour, tell us what you saw when you were on supervisory duty before Lily DeLuca left the school grounds."

"I saw a man standing by the school fence," Nicole said. "He had a small dog on a leash and was speaking with a group of students."

"Can you describe him?" Ryan asked.

"No," Nicole said. "I couldn't see his face because he was

wearing a baseball cap. I don't know if he was the same man I'd seen before."

"Can you describe the other man you've seen?"

"I'm sorry, I can't. He was far away, and the children blocked my view."

"What happened after?"

Nicole wrung her hands. "I was worried. I didn't like the way the man was talking to the children, so I ran over to take a photo of him." She glanced at me to subtly indicate she'd taken my advice.

"Were you able to get a photo?" Ryan asked her.

"Yes." She retrieved her phone from her jacket and tapped a few keys. "He took off when he saw me. I'm afraid the photo is blurry." Her hand shook as she held out her phone to him.

He studied the photo. "Can you send it to my email address, please?" He gave her his business card.

Her hand shaking, it took two tries before Nicole tapped the correct keys on her phone. "Okay. I sent it."

Ryan went on. "Miss Latour, did you see Lily DeLuca among the students talking to the stranger today?"

Nicole shrugged. "I can't say for sure. There were seven, maybe ten, students near the fence at the time. After the man left, I told the children to move away from there. I reminded them not to talk to strangers, no matter how friendly they were."

"Did you see Lily DeLuca leave the school premises?"

"No. My class was starting. I had to go back inside."

Ryan switched his attention to Miss Lombardi. "You had returned to the schoolyard by then?"

"Yes," she said. "I arrived seconds before Nicole, I mean Miss Latour, left. We make sure there's at least one teacher supervising the students at all times."

"Of course." Mrs. Alderwood smiled in agreement. After a pause in the conversation, she asked Ryan, "Do you have any other questions?"

"Not at the moment." Ryan pulled out another business card and handed it to the principal. "Thank you for your time. If any more details come to light, please call me."

"I certainly will." Mrs. Alderwood rose to her feet, prompting the rest of us to do the same.

Tears streamed silently down Miss Lombardi's cheeks as she came up to Ryan and me. "I am truly, truly sorry. I hope you find that sweet child." She dabbed at her face with a tissue and walked out.

As Nicole slipped past Ryan and me, she said, "Thank you."

Mrs. Alderwood approached us. "Lily DeLuca's parents are waiting for you in the visitors' room. I'll escort you there."

Anxiety intensified the knots in my stomach. I'd assisted Ryan in interviewing Vicky Johnson's parents, but the years had transformed their anxiety into grief and an acceptance that Vicky might not return. I was able to cope with that. It was a different experience from the one I was about to encounter.

Sitting in the same room as the DeLuca parents would test my ability to stay strong in the presence of extreme anguish. It would be difficult to control my reactions in the company of parents who were so distressed about their young daughter's recent disappearance. If a stranger had persuaded Lily to leave the safety of the schoolyard, her parents were right to be fearful about the horrid things that might have happened to her.

The range of their mixed emotions would filter through me and become my emotions. I might get an impression of Lily in the worst-case scenario and struggle to hide the terror of it from everyone else.

Was I ready for this?

22

———————

After a short walk along the main corridor of Blessed Mary Elementary School, Mrs. Alderwood opened the door to the visitors' room where an anxious mother and father sat waiting for us.

The DeLucas stood up as we entered. The angst they were suffering hung heavy in the air around us, tightening the space in the room. I fingered the crystal in my pocket to gain a few moments of calm.

After Mrs. Alderwood introduced us, she said to Ryan, "Please keep me informed of any developments." She left and closed the door behind her.

The distress that veiled Mr. DeLuca's face changed to expectancy. "Do you have any news?" he eagerly asked as we joined them at the table.

"Not yet, but I assure you that police teams are looking for Lily," Ryan said. "Right now, I'd like to ask you a few questions. How long has Lily been attending this school?"

"Several months," Mr. DeLuca said. "We're new to the neighborhood. Lily is our only child."

"Has Lily ever expressed how she felt about the school? Ever talked about any of her friends?"

"Lily is very sociable," Mrs. DeLuca said. "She was sad to leave our old home, but she adapted. She made new friends here quickly and adores her teachers."

"Would she have spoken to a stranger who might have tried to converse with her by the schoolyard fence?"

"No, not Lily. We often warned her not to speak to strangers, no matter where she was. She told us the teachers warned the students."

"Lily is a smart girl," her husband said. "She wouldn't talk to strangers. She wouldn't leave the school for no reason either."

I empathized with the DeLucas. Their agony was intense and weighed heavy on me. No parent should have to worry about whether or not a maniac lured their child away.

As I placed a hand gently on Mrs. DeLuca's arm, Lily's smiling face came to mind. "You can be sure we'll find your daughter and bring her back to you safely," I said, trying to allay her fears.

Ryan cleared his throat, then said to the DeLucas, "Since the first hours are critical, we've extended our coverage to law enforcement at all levels. From what you tell me, unless someone persuaded Lily to leave the school, it would be difficult to take her without her showing any resistance."

"She's a fighter," Mr. DeLuca said, smiling with pride. "And she runs fast. Very fast."

His wife turned to him. "She doesn't know the neighborhood. Where would she run to?"

"Lily is smart," Mr. DeLuca repeated. "She would kick and scream for help if she had to."

Holding back the tears, his wife pleaded with Ryan and me, "Please find our little girl."

Ryan buckled his seat belt with a hard snap and said, "I wish you wouldn't go making empty promises you can't keep, Amber. What if the DeLucas never see their daughter alive again?"

"It wasn't an empty promise," I retorted. "I based my statement on an insight I got. Their daughter will be found safe."

"You'd better be right." Without another word, he drove out of the school parking lot.

Ryan's brooding bothered me. I questioned whether he doubted me or whether I'd already failed in his view. That would be a logical deduction, one that would reduce my self-esteem for a short while. No, something else was bothering him, something that had nothing to do with me. Unfortunately, I had no idea what it was.

Since I had questions about Lily DeLuca, I appealed to his knowledge as a profiler. "If Lily's disappearance was an abduction, could it mean that we might have a new perpetrator in the area?"

Ryan nodded so-so. "It could also mean that a former perp was burnt out, took a break, and is now making a comeback. It's a rare occurrence, though."

"A twenty-year break?"

He steered the car around a corner. "Are you thinking he could be one of our three suspects in the Cinderella case?"

I answered with caution. "Maybe, but we don't have much to go on so far."

"The sighting of a man with a small dog might be a coincidence. Regardless, I have a hard time not connecting the guy to Tony Bruneau."

My image of an injured Tony was still sharp. "He's missing, and we don't know what happened to him. I've said this before. He could be in serious trouble."

"Trouble that he got himself into." Ryan's tone oozed with sarcasm. He parked the car on the street in front of a two-story home and cut the engine. "I'm counting on Gabriella Corti to tell us more about what she saw at the school." In an unexpected reversal of moods, he smiled at me and asked, "Would you like to handle the interview?"

Ryan and I took our seats in the Corti family's living room. Tightly holding a teddy bear, seven-year-old Gabriella huddled between her parents on the couch facing ours. A close friend of Lily DeLuca, she was the only witness who had seen the girl leave the school grounds this afternoon.

Ryan had surprised me when he suggested that I interview Gabriella. It wasn't as if he admired my communication skills or the way I perceived things about the people around me. No, he believed that the little girl would feel less intimidated if a woman asked the questions.

I spoke softly. "Gabriella, I understand you saw a man standing by the school fence today."

"Yes," she said.

"Can you tell me if this was the man you saw?" I tapped my phone and showed her a photo of Tony Bruneau.

She looked at it. "I don't know."

"Can you tell us anything about the man you saw by the fence?"

The girl glanced up at her mother.

"Go on, Gaby," Mrs. Corti said.

"He was scary," Gabriella whispered.

I prompted her. "Scary?"

She looked up at her mother again.

"Tell her about the puppy on the leash," her mother said to her.

"The man was giving away his puppy," Gabriella said. "He asked who wanted it. He said it was a golden kind."

I assumed she meant a golden retriever. "Did anyone want the puppy?"

"One of the girls said yes."

"Which girl?"

"I don't remember?"

"Was it Lily?"

"No, not Lily."

"Then what happened?"

Gabriella spoke faster. "The man said he forgot the puppy's bowl and toys at home. He told the girl she had to go with him."

"Did she go?"

"No, because I told her not to. Mommy said not to go with a stranger or something bad would happen to me."

"Your mommy is very smart." I smiled at Mrs. Corti. "And so are you, Gabriella."

The little girl offered a tense smile.

I went on. "Gabriella, did you see any other student leave with the man?"

"I don't know." Her lips quivered. "I'm scared the man will come back."

I leaned forward. "I promise you, Gabriella, he will not bother you or any of your friends again."

Ryan rapidly said, "About Lily DeLuca—"

I cut him off. "Gabriella, you saw your friend Lily walk out of the schoolyard at recess this afternoon. Is that right?"

"Yes," she said.

"Was she alone?"

"Yes."

"What did you do?"

"I shouted, 'Lily, come back,' but she didn't listen. I wasn't allowed to leave the school, so I ran to tell the teacher." She started to cry.

Gabriella's anxiety about her missing friend was heartbreaking. I wanted to comfort her and tell her that things would work out fine, but I didn't. Ryan had already signaled that I'd gone too far.

As we walked back to the car in silence, I sensed the anger bubbling inside him like a volcano about to erupt. I suspected he was going to rebuke me for making that promise to Gabriella. And I was right.

"You did it again, Amber." He tightened his hands on the steering wheel. "Why did you feel justified in making that promise to Gabriella?"

"Did you see how scared she was? I was trying to put her at ease. Besides, it's the truth. Lily won't be harmed."

He raised his hands in the air. "It's not as if you're an all-seeing superpower. How can you be so sure?"

I ignored the slight and put on a brave front. "Because I trust my feelings."

Ryan shrugged and started the engine.

"Where are we going next?"

"To speak with people who live near Blessed Mary Elementary School. Let's hope your feelings will help you find a resident who saw something suspicious."

He had a right not to trust my gift. Sometimes I wasn't sure I trusted it myself.

23

It wasn't until we'd interviewed the last resident in the vicinity of Blessed Mary Elementary School that our efforts produced a lead. According to Ernie Baker's testimony, a teenager had recently stopped by the schoolyard fence.

"He could have a kid brother or sister at the school," the senior told Ryan and me. "He comes by often enough."

"How often?" Ryan asked.

He adjusted his bifocals. "At least twice in the last week. He plays baseball with his friends most afternoons in the park nearby. I see him there when I take my daily walk."

"Can you describe him?"

"About seventeen years old. On the slim side. A little stooped like me." He chuckled. "If you hurry, you'll catch up to him."

～

Ryan parked the car on the street, and we hurried into the park.

My pulse sped up. Ernie Baker's description of the boy was familiar. I had a feeling we were about to meet up with the real-life version of the young man we'd seen in Mr. Caron's home video.

We soon spotted a group of teenage boys holding baseball bats and mitts. After they parted ways, one of them headed in our direction. His hunched stance and the way he walked were sure giveaways.

I kept my voice low. "Ryan, that's him...the boy who delivered the second slipper to the Johnson home!"

Ryan pulled out his badge as the youth neared. "Can we have a few words with you?"

The boy stopped. "About what?"

"What's your name?"

"Theo."

"How old are you?"

"Eighteen."

"Theo, do you know any students who go to Blessed Mary Elementary School?"

"No."

"Do you make it a habit to stop and talk to the children in the schoolyard?"

"No."

"A witness saw you there."

Theo's gaze bit into him. "So what? It's not a crime, is it?"

"A little girl went missing from that school today," I said. "Police are looking for her."

The teen raised his hands. "No! I had nothing to do with that. I was just doing some old dude a favor."

"What old dude?" Ryan asked.

"Some dude. Hell, I don't know his name. He gave me twenty bucks to go talk to some little kids. That's all."

"Can you describe him?"

"I'm not good with faces." He looked down.

"Did he pay you to do other things for him?"

Theo kicked a pebble and remained silent.

"Where do you live?"

He tightened his lips. "Around here."

The fear radiating from the boy was real yet perplexing. His evasive and somewhat bold replies showed he wasn't afraid of the police. What or who was he afraid of?

Ryan pulled out his business card. "Here's my info. If you remember anything else about the man, give me a call."

The last place I wanted to be this evening was cooped up in a police station with Ryan. My ego was still suffering from the verbal lashing he'd given me after our interview with the Corti family. Specifically, *my* interview with Gabriella, their seven-year-old daughter.

A glimmer of optimism raised my spirits about another case, though. The Cinderella commercial about Vicky Johnson was scheduled to launch during a news broadcast at dinnertime. I joined Lieutenant Payton, Ryan, and Nadia in the conference room to watch it on TV. With Vicky's video playing over numerous media channels, we expected a positive response from the public.

It was all there. Vicky's photos as a child, the age-progression sketches, background history... The commercial had a compassionate appeal to it. Now all we had to do was wait for someone to come forward with a solid lead.

"Excellent work," the lieutenant said as the video ended.

He was about to leave when a news clip about the local disappearance of Lily DeLuca immediately followed. The reporter commented:

"We have to question whether Vicky Johnson's abduction twenty years ago is connected to today's Amber alert regarding the disappearance of seven-year-old Lily DeLuca. It's a known fact that police have recently revisited the Vicky Johnson case while hundreds of other missing persons cases in the Montreal area remain unsolved. How many more children have been abducted over the past decades? And why have police investigators been so lax in warning the public about a potential serial killer who might be prowling the streets of the city?"

"Oh, terrific!" the lieutenant raged. "The media is going to cause a public uproar with this. Why did they have to go and say, 'serial killer'?"

Shaken, I said, "If Lily's parents heard this reporter's comment, it'll crush their hope that their daughter will be found alive."

"Lieutenant, do you want us to prepare an additional message for the media?" Ryan asked.

"No, it'll fan the flames and make matters worse. I'm heading home. You know how to reach me."

I canceled my evening visit to the retirement home so I could take my share of calls on the Info-Crime line. Sitting at my desk, I slouched behind my computer, thankful that it formed a barrier between Ryan and me. The less I spoke to that man, the better.

My cell phone rang.

It was Nicole. "Hello, there, Amber." Her playful tone danced across the line.

I would have bet anything that the topic was going to be Ryan. I glanced over at his desk, relieved to see that he was on the phone. "Hi, Nicole," I whispered.

"Are you at work? Can you talk?"

"Yes, to the first question. Not for long, to the second question."

"Okay. I'll make it fast." A mini cyclone of words spilled out of her mouth. "I couldn't wait to tell you how handsome Ryan is. You didn't tell me you assisted him in investigations."

"Um...sometimes. We'll have to talk about this another time."

"Okay. I get it. He's hanging around your desk."

"Yes."

"I'll call you later. When do you get home?"

"I don't know. It could be very late."

"I'll call you tomorrow then. Sweet dreams, Amber!"

The phones in the outer office began to ring moments later. Nadia and Corey, another recent recruit in communications, weeded incoming calls to eliminate curiosity seekers who had seen the Cinderella video. They told reporters that the police had no additional information at the time.

I tried to envision what had happened to Tony and Lily DeLuca. It was a useless attempt. My impressions arrived when they chose to, not when I wanted them to.

As the evening wore on, more calls came in, but no concrete leads. Nadia and Corey handled the callers expertly right up to the end of their shift when two rookie officers arrived to replace them.

Bored yet hopeful, I reviewed Vicky Johnson's case file again in case something might pop out at me. Who was I kidding? I knew the file inside out. The only thing missing was evidence. Solid evidence.

Since we couldn't leave our posts, going out for dinner was out of the question. I did the next best thing and opted to get a cup of coffee in the kitchen.

Politeness prevailed. "Ryan, would you like some coffee?"

"Sure," he said.

Luckily, someone had had the forethought to make a fresh pot. I returned with the cups and handed him one.

"Thanks." He smiled briefly. "It's not very promising so far, is it?"

I wasn't in the mood for chitchat, especially with him. "It's early yet." I strolled back to my desk, feeling his eyes on me.

The phone rang on the Info-Crime line, breaking the stillness in the station.

Ryan pounced on it. After he listened to an inquisitive

caller, he went into an explanation of something in Vicky's video.

Another line buzzed and I picked it up.

"You and your cop buddies are inept," a robotic voice said.

"Excuse me?"

"You honestly think the Cinderella video is going to help you solve the case?"

Although he used a phone app, I was certain it was a man's voice. "Who is this?"

He ignored my question. "You truly believe that witnesses will open up to you, Amber, of all people?"

He knew my name!

My pulse increased. It was him! Vicky's abductor!

I tried to keep my voice steady. "You don't know anything about me."

"You're so wrong," he sneered. "You lived with that poor excuse for a family until you finally decided to take an apartment on your own."

He knew where I lived!

"You read to dead people or people who have death knocking at their door. Including those poor, sick children. You see, Amber, I've been keeping an eye on you for years."

A memory from the night my parents were murdered suddenly rushed back:

The night-light in my room cast a faint glow on the man. He was standing and wiping his sweaty face with a gloved hand.

The caller—it was him! The man who killed my parents!

I stifled a gasp and fumbled for the crystal in my jacket pocket, holding it firmly. "I know who you are."

"I doubt it, or you would have caught up to me by now. If you think you can solve the Cinderella case, you're mistaken. Take my advice. Stop poking around, or you'll regret it."

I tried to conjure up an image of the caller but couldn't. Something was preventing me. Instead, I captured another insight:

A man was chasing young children in a forest. They were screaming and tripping in the darkness, the horror on their faces visible in the moonlight.

"Playing the silent game, are we?" he said, misinterpreting my pause. "Face it. You're a loser in every way, Amber. No friends. No lover. Your aunt and uncle felt sorry you were an orphan and tossed you a crumb once in a while, like co-signing for the purchase of your car. Not that it helped your career. You're lousy on the job too."

Panic engulfed me. Laura had warned me about this monster. He was trying to destroy my self-confidence and make me question my capabilities.

I swallowed hard and mustered up as much confidence as I could. "We'll find you, and you'll pay for what you've done. It's only a matter of time."

He snickered. "You don't have time on your side. There's a lot more of them out there."

The line went dead.

Shocked by the caller's disclosures and still clutching the receiver, I rose from my chair on unsteady legs. "Ryan!"

24

Ryan scrambled to my desk, his eyes searching mine. "What happened?"

Still holding the receiver, I struggled to breathe normally. "It was him...Vicky's abductor! He just called!" My mind reeled with a horrid prospect. "What if he kidnapped Lily DeLuca from school today? And here we are, running around in circles looking for Tony Bruneau. We have to find this lunatic before he kills Lily!"

His forehead puckered. "Get a grip, Amber! We're doing all we can with the information we have. Maybe you should try harder to be the badass you were meant to be!"

"I can't!"

He studied me as if he were debating whether or not he'd pushed the matter too far. In a calmer voice, he said, "Let me listen to the recording."

"Please don't put it on speakerphone." As he gently pried my fingers from the receiver, the perception of a car crashing into a concrete wall almost threw me off my feet. "Oh, no!"

"What is it?"

"I can't explain it. I perceived a terrible car accident. The occupant was dead."

Ryan blinked. "What?"

Confused by the inexplicable images that had bombarded me, I waved a hand in dismissal. "The car crash...forget it. It's crazy."

What was happening to me? Had the caller disturbed me so much that he'd thrown my psyche off balance? Was I starting to envision ridiculous thoughts that had nothing to do with the Cinderella case? With my parents' case?

While Ryan listened to the recording, uneasiness seeped through me. He'd hear how the caller branded me a loser and a loner. He'd learn intimate details about me, my family, and my private life.

Ryan's expression changed from disbelief to apprehension as the recording came to an end. He set the receiver down. "He seems to know a lot of personal things about you. Are they true?"

"It's true that I'm adopted," I said, skirting the other issues.

"I'm sorry. I didn't know."

"I didn't expect you to know." I wanted to tell him that my parents had been murdered and that I was reviewing their file, but there was so much riding on that great reveal. What if he found out that Chief Tremblay was my uncle? Worse, what if he thought I'd used my connection to get the consultant job? It would wipe out any scrap of confidence he'd shown in my abilities until now.

Yet I took this latest call to the Info-Crime line as a sign that it was time to come clean with Ryan if I wanted to find my parents' killer. I could tell him the truth and leave out a detail, like who my adoptive parents were. Again, I was worrying for nothing. There was no photo of Uncle Ted in the file.

"There's something else you should know about me," I said. "My parents were murdered. I've been going through their cold case file." I pulled it out from under a stack of papers and handed it to him. "I'm sure the mystery caller is the same man who killed them and tried to abduct me twenty years ago."

Astounded, Ryan slowly leafed through the reports and photos without saying a word, then placed the file on my desk. "You should have told me sooner, Amber."

"Why? What difference would it have made? I'm not asking for sympathy."

"That's not what I meant, though I feel horrible about what happened. The point is, I referred this file to the lieutenant initially. He argued against following up on it. I didn't understand his refusal and didn't make the connection to you until now. It must be painful for you." His dark eyes reflected compassion.

"Please don't tell the lieutenant. I might not have another opportunity to try to solve my parents' case."

He hesitated, thinking. "Okay. Since you feel so strongly about the caller's identity, we'll keep your parents' case at hand while we work on Vicky's."

Relief flowed through me. "Thanks. I'd like that."

Whether out of politeness or a respect for my privacy, Ryan went back to discussing the anonymous caller. "Did you get any other thoughts regarding a name or description?"

"I tried but couldn't," I said. "Where has he been hiding all this time?"

"Good question. He said, 'there's a lot more of them out there.' It's possible he meant more victims."

"I don't know. All I got was a man chasing frightened children through a dark forest."

He arched an eyebrow. "Imagine how the public would react if they knew more children had died at the hands of this perp? After his bold call tonight, we might be closer to the truth than we know."

"What if it means he's accelerating his killings?" Horrific

acts that the perpetrator might have inflicted on his young victims triggered my imagination. Repulsion swelled inside me. I reached for the crystal in my pocket to contain my feelings and slow down my racing heart.

Ryan peered at me. "You look pale, Amber. Can I get you some water?"

"No. I'm okay."

He gently touched my arm. "Are you sure?"

His concern surprised yet comforted me. "Yes." I took a sip of my cold coffee.

"Don't let him get to you. He's bragging. He's taunting us with a *come and catch me, if you can* message."

"He wants attention."

"Exactly. It fits the profile."

"Can you trace the call?"

"No," Ryan said. "These guys are smart. They use burner phones, then ditch them. Untraceable." He passed a hand over the stubble on his chin. "The timing of his call is interesting. I think the Cinderella video triggered it."

"It makes sense, except..."

"Except what?"

"He must know that I have access to other case files." I placed a hand on my parents' file as if to protect the contents.

"Here's my theory," he said. "In his bizarre, demented world, the perp could be interpreting our work as admiration for the gruesome acts he considered his lifetime achievements. He's ecstatic that someone is finally giving his victims the attention they deserved after all these years. He insulted you only to boost his self-esteem."

"More victims means he might be behind more cold cases." I eyed the pile of bankers boxes by my desk and wished I had the time to delve into each file.

Ryan reached for his phone. "I'll send the lieutenant an urgent text message. He has to know about this latest call."

After he sent the message, he glanced at his watch. "We've been at this for hours. I doubt your mystery guy will call back tonight. Let's take a break and go get dinner. My treat. If another lead comes in through the Info-Crime line, the staff will contact us."

25

Even at nine in the evening, people were drifting into Sam's Diner from the adjoining poolroom. I hadn't visited this late-night eatery, but Ryan assured me it was one of the best diners in town.

The service, however, wasn't up to par. When the breaded codfish arrived, I refused it. I explained to the attendant that it was a mistake and that I'd ordered a chicken salad.

"I'll have it," Ryan said. "I'm hungry enough to eat both." He gestured to his plate of hamburger and fries.

While he talked about how he'd skipped meals on the job, a panhandler in a cap, grubby jacket, and jeans went up to the back counter where the attendant collected the meals ready to be served. A moment later, a staff manager twice the man's size approached him and escorted him out of the diner.

I was about to mention the incident but changed my mind. I sensed the eagerness behind Ryan's words and didn't want to interrupt him.

"When I was young, my dad used to take the family out for dinner every weekend," he said, smiling, surprising me with his candor. "It gave my mom a break. She had enough to do the rest of the week with five of us running around. She had a tough life. I'm glad she's living comfortably now."

"And your father?"

A cloud skimmed over his face. "My dad died when I was a teenager. It's bad enough having to deal with the usual stuff when we're young but losing our parents..." His voice trailed off and he swiftly changed the subject. "I was lucky to have siblings and we supported one another. I couldn't see myself in your situation. Growing up alone, I mean."

I valued the sincerity behind his words, yet I refused to be pitied. "Oh no, my aunt and uncle were very generous with their time. They spoiled me with trips and gifts..." I hastily added, "Of course, I went out with friends...had parties...the usual stuff, growing up."

White lies. My birthday parties with other children were cut short. Their lively emotions overwhelmed me. I refused most invitations to go out with teenage friends, and later, coworkers because I absorbed the energy of crowds around me. If I did accept the occasional outing, I'd come home exhausted and with a headache.

"Since we're getting personal, does your name have anything to do with your...um...talent?" Ryan asked.

"My mom named me Amber because she said no two gemstones were identical, that I was special and had a keen ability. I didn't know what she meant until I was in primary school and could feel the sadness and joy in my classmates."

"Feeling someone else's emotions... That sounds intrusive to me."

"It can be." Uneasy about discussing my gift, I moved on to another topic. "Speaking of the past, I often dream about my parents' old home." He didn't have to know that my dreams were actually nightmares. "I was a child and didn't say a proper goodbye to it."

"Same here," he said. "You get attached to a place, even if you only spend a few years living there. My dad was in the military, so we relocated often. I didn't get a chance to say goodbye to the houses we left behind."

The attendant arrived with my chicken salad and placed it before me. "Enjoy." She gave me a perky smile, then left.

I stayed on topic. "If we don't say goodbye to our old home, it's as if we haven't truly shut the door behind us."

"I agree," Ryan said. "In hindsight, I wished I'd looked in each room one last time to store it in my memory. In most cases, though, I was too young to think about doing that." He took a bite of the codfish.

"I legally own my parents' old house, so I can visit it once the current renters leave."

He smiled. "You can finally say goodbye to it."

My reason for visiting my old home was different. I wanted to see if I could sense any vibes about the killer, though I wasn't prepared to share that with Ryan yet.

"What about your life outside work?" he asked.

"My volunteer jobs keep me busy." I told him about my periodic visits to the children's hospital and to retirement homes. "By the way, I love visiting with your mother. She's so sweet."

"Yeah, she's doing okay. Some days she remembers me. Others, she doesn't." Again, a shadow crossed his face. He took another bite of the codfish.

His vulnerability revealed a new side to him that I hadn't seen before. Like me, he'd suffered the loss of his father at a young age and now his mother's memory was fading. That his mother didn't know who he was at times could explain his occasional brooding episodes.

I had to admit that having dinner with Ryan was beginning to alter my views about him. Sharing our common background was a surprising change from our usual competitive bantering.

Although our relationship was basically a working one, I welcomed this new aspect of it.

"Speaking of free time," Ryan said, redirecting the conversation once more, "my friends hound me on my days off, so I have no choice but to socialize more." He chuckled. "They help me to relax and forget about the sad parts of my life, so that's a positive thing. What do you do to relax?"

His question flustered me, and I dug into my plate. "I only have a few close friends. I prefer it that way."

"I've been there," he said. "Sometimes you think you'll never get over the pain, but you do. After my father died, I built a barrier around myself as a safeguard. Things changed as the years went by. I learned that I was merely hurting myself by pushing others away. So, I stopped being afraid of losing anyone else. Instead, I opened up and trusted people more."

His message, though subtle, was meant for me. "Trust. It goes both ways, doesn't it?" I ate a forkful of my chicken salad.

"What do you mean?"

"You trust them to let them into your life, and they trust you."

Ryan held my gaze. "Ah, I know what this is about. You think I don't trust you. Or is it the other way around?"

"We use different tools, but our goal is the same," I said. "Mutual trust benefits the arrangement."

"I'll be straight with you." He put his fork down. "I focus on the facts, so I was skeptical about your abilities at first. Now I believe your insights might be beneficial after all. I respect that." He gave me a warm smile.

A sensation rippled through me, stirring tender emotions. Was that affection I sensed from Ryan? "Why the sudden turnaround?"

"The perceptions that you get... If we can connect the dots between them and specific aspects of the crimes..." He put a hand on his throat. "I'm not feeling so good." He clumsily retrieved an EpiPen inside his pocket. Before he could use it, he keeled over, sending a plate crashing to the floor.

I bolted from my seat, grabbed the EpiPen, and stabbed his thigh. I pulled out my phone and dialed 9-1-1, then sent Lieutenant Payton his second urgent text message of the day.

26

———————

His brow furrowed with worry, Lieutenant Payton hurried into the waiting room of the hospital emergency ward. "Any news?" He unzipped his jacket and sat in the chair next to me.

I felt as frantic as he looked. "No, nothing yet."

"It's not like Ryan to be careless about his food allergies. Good thing he had an EpiPen with him."

"They're running tests. They don't know for sure that it was a food allergy."

"What else could it be?"

I hadn't forgotten about the panhandler who was evicted from the diner after he'd loitered by the serving area. What if he were the killer in disguise and had quickly sprinkled poison over Ryan's food?

No, it didn't make sense. He would have targeted me instead. A minor detail escaped my attention, but I couldn't put my finger on it...

It suddenly surfaced. "Ryan ate the fish meal that was originally intended for me." I explained how the attendant had brought the dish to our table by mistake and that Ryan had offered to eat it anyway. I mentioned my suspicion about the panhandler, then retracted it. The idea now seemed far-fetched.

The lieutenant pondered my words. "Let's wait and see what the doctor has to say."

"Have you notified Ryan's family?"

"No. I don't want to upset his mother until we get a medical diagnosis. She took it hard when his father died in a horrible car crash. Ryan was just a teenager then."

A car crash! That explained it. When Ryan took the receiver out of my hand at the station, I'd caught a glimpse into his world. Why hadn't he told me his father had died in a car accident?

The lieutenant had something else on his mind. "Amber, fill me in about the anonymous call you got. Ryan sent me a text message, but I'd like to hear your thoughts about it."

I briefed him, omitting the insults that the caller had hurled at me. "He knew personal facts about me. That's scary."

"The fact that he knew you were adopted..." He pursed his lips. "That disturbs me." The lines in his brow deepened. "Sometimes we can let our imagination run wild when we're faced with a challenging case. In your situation, my gut tells me the danger truly exists."

I had a strange feeling he was about to disclose a deep secret.

"Amber, I know that Chief Tremblay is your uncle. We've worked together for many years, and I trust his judgment implicitly. That's why I accepted his recommendation to bring you on board." In response to my troubled stare, he added, "It's okay. Your secret is safe with me."

"Thank you." My attention swung to the doctor approaching us at a fast clip, a stethoscope hanging from his neck.

"Ryan appears to be in no immediate danger," the doctor said. "We suspect he had an allergic reaction to something he ate."

"Can we see him?" the lieutenant asked.

"We're running tests, so it could take a while. In the meantime, we'll keep Ryan here overnight for observation." He hastily excused himself and moved on to continue his rounds.

The lieutenant zipped up his jacket. "No use waiting around. Can I give you a ride home, Amber?"

"My car is at the station. Can you drive me back there instead? I'd like to update some files."

"I'll drive you there and escort you home afterward."

"You really don't have—"

"I insist. Besides, I should pop into the station. Maybe the QPP got lucky in their search for Vicky's remains in Larkland Park."

The staff would have contacted him if anything important had developed. Driving me around at this time of the night was merely an excuse to make sure I'd be safe. For my Uncle Ted's sake.

The Info-Crime line had received several witness accounts about Lily DeLuca. One caller claimed he'd seen the seven-year-old girl on a busy downtown street. Another had spotted her with two adults in a restaurant. A third caller had seen her in a nearby grocery store.

The reports bordered on absurd. If Lily's parents believed their daughter was cautious, she wouldn't have wandered along Montreal streets alone at night or willingly gone to a restaurant with total strangers. And if she had wandered into a grocery store, she would have asked someone there for help.

I shared my findings with the lieutenant.

He had the same reservations. "Those are simple cases of wishful thinking. I'll get dispatch to send a patrol car to check out each lead, just in case."

Back at my desk, I opened up Vicky Johnson's website page

and links to relative social media sites. There were a few kind-hearted comments but no leads.

I closed my eyes and leaned back in the chair. The day's events were starting to take their toll on me. I used this quiet time to evaluate the progress we'd made—or hadn't—in tracking down Vicky's abductor.

We had evidence: White vans. Secret photos of young children. Fairy-tale books. Witness reports of strange men lurking near schoolyards.

About fairy-tale books... Anyone might argue that millions of fathers read storybooks to their children and grandfathers to their grandchildren. Did that make them child abductors?

A common thread was that our three suspects lived or had lived in the vicinity of Vicky's home. What if Vicky's abductor wasn't one of our three suspects? What if another abductor had kidnapped her?

It was useless. While Ryan and I had gathered new information, the same doubts about each suspect remained. A tip that had led us to Theo, the teen in the park, had been promising. Unfortunately, fear had prevented him from telling us more about the man who'd paid him to drop off Vicky's second slipper.

On a promising note, evidence might surface to incriminate an offender if the police search team found the girl's remains in Larkland Park. If not, how much longer would Ryan and I have before the lieutenant pulled the plug on our investigations?

My thoughts deviated to my parents' case. I wasn't selfish, but I believed it was high time to focus on my own demons. Today's anonymous caller knew a lot about my past. If he murdered my parents, could he be one of the three main suspects in Vicky's case? Or another unknown abductor?

I was going in circles.

Lieutenant Payton strolled up to my desk. "The QPP haven't located anything in Larkland Park so far. You ready to go home?"

"Yes." I grabbed my handbag and followed him out to the parking area, then got into my car. Although I objected, he insisted on following me home to ensure my safe arrival.

During the drive, I glanced at the rearview mirror from time to time. The lieutenant trailed me at a comfortable distance. I smiled to myself. His escort was unnecessary, though reassuring.

The ugly truth was that the killer was stalking me. And he knew where I lived!

My pulse picked up speed.

Paranoia was creeping up on me.

I soon arrived at my destination and parked in my allotted space. After I dashed into the building and unlocked the second glass door, I looked back outside. The lieutenant was parked on the street and had waited until I was safely inside. He flashed his headlights, then drove off.

Sitting in my living room, I had an impulse to call Ryan at the hospital but changed my mind. He might be sleeping, and I didn't want to disturb him.

I replayed our conversation at the diner and how we'd shared personal memories. Exchanging similar stories about our family backgrounds made me feel as if our relationship were a normal one. Seeing a friendlier side of Ryan instead of his brooding was an improvement. Deep down, he was kind and had a good heart. And he was definitely handsome. It would be exciting if a romantic relationship developed between us.

I stopped. It suddenly dawned on me that I'd allowed Ryan to enter my private world.

Big mistake.

There was no way I'd ever let anyone get close to me again. The pain I'd suffered when I lost my parents forced me to build a wall of defense around me. I wasn't about to let it crumble because I chose to let someone become a special part of my life.

Especially Ryan. If I didn't allow myself to open up to him, then I wouldn't fall in love with him, and my heart wouldn't break when he left me. I promised myself that I would keep my love locked up tight and not open my heart to anyone from now on.

Yes, I'd have to be more careful with Ryan in the future.

27

———————

I set out early the next morning to see Laura. With Ryan in the hospital, I was at a standstill in Vicky Johnson's investigation. Time had become a precious commodity. The pressure to solve the case meant that I needed more insight into the inner workings of the perpetrator I was dealing with. My psychologist confidante was my last hope.

Taking my usual seat in Laura's office, I updated her about my conversation with the anonymous caller and my suspicions. "I'm sure he's the man who killed my parents and tried to kidnap me."

"My heavens!" Laura blinked in surprise.

"What can you tell me about him?"

She joined her hands, thinking. "From what you said about him, he displayed no fear, only bravado, which perhaps increased after he got away with a number of crimes. I'm glad to hear you showed no fear."

"I doubt I was that convincing. To be honest, he caught me off guard. I'm sure he's been stalking me because he knew all about my apartment, my family, my job—"

"A word of caution." She raised a forefinger. "Pedophiles are manipulators. As a manipulator, he knows how to flatter others with his wit and charm. Likewise, how to humiliate them when he discovers their weaknesses."

"You're right about the last part." I repeated fragments of the demeaning conversation I'd had with the caller. "Believe me, he didn't send any compliments my way."

"That's because he knows your strengths but chooses to ignore them," Laura pointed out. "Manipulators study people to determine their weaknesses and gain power over them. What he did was focus on your vulnerabilities. It's an easy next step to exploit them and attack."

I was astounded. "My vulnerabilities? How would he know what my vulnerabilities were?"

"In your case, the trauma of losing your parents created an emptiness inside you, perhaps conveyed as a lack of self-confidence. A manipulator would seize that as a vulnerability. It seems to me that he's already taken the first steps toward his goal."

"Back up a minute. How would he know anything about my self-confidence...or lack of it?"

"Generally speaking, he's aware that you've led a sheltered life and that you restrict your interactions to a limited circle of people. He's also aware that you choose jobs in safe one-on-one environments. In other words, you're not a social butterfly. He interprets your behavior as a weakness and is trying to transfer his own weakness to you by demeaning you."

I had more questions. "What do you mean by 'transfer his own weakness to me'?"

Laura spoke softly. "I don't want to frighten you, but this is my theory. You might have been among his first abduction attempts, if not his first. You might have been his first failure as well. He doesn't like to be reminded of it. Your existence does that."

"Terrific." I raised my hands in the air, then let them land with a thump in my lap. "I'm sure it won't be my last conversation with him. What can I expect?"

"Understand that every situation is about him. He's cunning, careful, and organized. He needs to win, no matter how difficult the challenge."

"I get it. So, what can I say to him? I don't know anything about him."

"If he calls, it means he wants to talk," Laura said. "Let him talk and then rebuff his statements."

I was at a loss. "How can I do that?"

"He might brag about his accomplishments to you. Abductors and murderers are known to do that. If his crimes date back decades, it means he's managed to evade the police all this time. Consequently, he's overconfident about what he has achieved and enjoys boasting about his deeds, even to other killers. Use real facts to destroy his base by destroying his beliefs about himself."

"How can I draw him out?"

Laura sat back. "I'm not sure that you can. That is, unless he wants to be found. However, as I mentioned the last time, he might be craving the spotlight in his older years, but I doubt he'll want to show his face for obvious reasons. It's more likely that he wants to be admired from afar as someone who succeeded in making the police look like fools."

I shook my head in frustration. "There must be a way to find him."

"One possibility is that he might return to places where he committed the crimes. Abductors do that when their egos get in the way of common sense. Otherwise, they're great escape artists."

"It depends on the crime, doesn't it? Why would he go back to a place if the victim is no longer there?"

Laura gathered several pens by her notepad. "Revisiting a place where he successfully committed a crime brings back the memory and the excitement of the act itself. In his mind, he

relives the moment and feels the same thrill as he did originally. He has no empathy whatsoever for his victims. As I said
earlier, you represent his failure. He is extremely interested in
enacting revenge on you."

"Why come after me now? Is it because I'm working on
certain cold cases?"

"In his twisted way, he sees any police investigation that
might implicate him as an injustice. After all, the media has
painted him as a criminal who stole innocent children from
their parents. Negative public opinion goes against his self-
image as a protector."

"The public is right. He *is* a criminal."

"All the more reason to be aware of your surroundings.
Child abductors and adult abductors have different prefer-
ences, yet the motivations can be similar: domination, control,
and sexual desire. The latter is fairly common."

I cringed. "Are you saying he's going to try to abduct me
again?"

"Perhaps figuratively," Laura said. "Right now, it's all about
gaining control over you or getting rid of you. Like most manipulators, he has a warped sense of authority and blames others
when things go wrong. He takes no responsibility for his
actions and will angrily deflect and threaten anyone who questions him. He enjoys inflicting pain on others. In this case, his
target is you."

"Thanks for the warning." I considered the irony of the situation. "The fact that he bases his kidnapping motives on innocent fairy tales is so repulsive."

"The genre of fairy tales is getting darker," Laura said with a
sigh. "They were originally about hopeful stories through
which we got acquainted with monsters. They helped us to
solve life's problems later on. Today, it's as if fairy tales are
trying to keep in step with the rest of the world's ugly and
alarming events."

"For me, the ugliness began the night my parents were murdered."

She leaned slightly forward. "You know, Amber, you could be harboring other clues about that night. Perhaps your mind is working as a protective device and has chosen not to reveal something of a disturbing nature to you. Stay open to possibilities that things might not appear as they seem."

"I will, but how can I solve this case if I can't get inside the killer's head?"

"Don't be afraid to ask for help. From what you've told me, your partner, Ryan, sounds trustworthy. You can rely on him." She checked the time. "One last word of advice. Your guilt about not having saved your parents can create a doubt about your psychic abilities and your efforts to investigate cases. Ignore it. Try to appreciate your gift as one would value any other talent. Allow yourself to trust it. Remember how strong and brave you are to have survived so much."

I thanked her, gave her a hug, and left.

Laura was right. I had to trust my instincts and find a way to catch the killer. I refused to be vulnerable to his attacks, verbal or otherwise. I'd strengthen the wall of protection around me to evade his insults and threats. Most of all, I vowed to work through my fears and develop a plan to bring this devious maniac to justice without becoming his next target.

No matter what it took.

28

The three leads about Lily DeLuca that we'd received through the Info-Crime line hadn't panned out. Police interviews disclosed that the incidents were either bogus, or the witnesses were mistaken in identifying the missing seven-year-old girl.

Like the lieutenant, I wasn't surprised. What did surprise me was seeing Ryan stroll into the station and pull up a chair across from my desk later that morning.

"I didn't expect you'd be back at work so soon," I said. "You looked a little gray last night."

"That's exactly how I felt," he said. "It turned out to be an allergy to the homemade sauce at the restaurant. It contained bits of shrimp, which is my worst food allergy. I should have asked about it first." With a sheepish smile, he added, "Thank you for...you know...the EpiPen."

"Hey, I'd have done it for anyone."

"Oh. And here I thought I was special." He chuckled, then grew serious. "No, honestly. Your quick action proves that I can trust you with my life."

His openness melted my heart. I felt sincere gratitude

emanating from him and something else. His lingering gaze gave me a warm feeling inside.

Ryan's phone pinged twice. He checked his messages. "Forensics confirmed they were unable to enhance the photo your teacher friend took in the schoolyard. A baseball cap hid a large part of the man's face, so they couldn't properly identify him."

"Nicole will be disappointed," I said. She'd left several messages on my cell phone, but I hadn't had the time to call her back.

"They did confirm the dog was a Golden retriever, though."

"Which could be Tony Bruneau's dog."

"Exactly." He tapped a few more keys. "You remember the unsourced video we viewed the other day? The one that dated back twenty years with George Simon and another guy walking into the police station?"

"Yes, yes. What about it?"

"Archives sent me a message." Ryan glanced at his phone. "The other guy the police interviewed was Lawrence Townsend. A potential witness. Since he wasn't considered a suspect in the Vicky Johnson case, investigators didn't record their meeting. The RCMP database shows there's nothing on file for him there either."

"Another dead end," I said.

Footsteps drew my attention.

"Good news!" Lieutenant Payton scuttled up to us, waving a sheet of paper. "They found Lily DeLuca!"

"That's a relief," I said.

"Where did they find her?" Ryan asked.

"Not far from her home." The lieutenant scanned the report. "She left the schoolyard at recess because she wasn't feeling well."

"Why didn't she tell the teacher on supervisory duty?"

"She said the teacher was busy moving students away from the fence."

"The teacher suspected an intruder had tried to approach the children," Ryan said. "She took a photo of the man. It was blurry and forensics couldn't enhance it."

"I see." The lieutenant went on. "Long story short, Lily got lost on her way home and fell asleep in a park behind a large tree. A woman found her when she went jogging at the crack of dawn and called the police."

Ryan stood up. "Are we sure that Lily's story is legit? That nothing happened to her in the interim?"

"They took her to the hospital. Her parents are with her."

"I should check if Tony Bruneau returned to his apartment." Ryan took a step toward his desk.

"Hold on," the lieutenant said to him. "The surveillance team just confirmed there's been no activity in Tony's apartment to date. He hasn't been seen in the area either."

The image of Tony's bruised body popped into my mind again. "Something must have happened to him. It's the only explanation."

~

Vicky Johnson's video produced a new witness. Jennie Fry had babysat the missing girl decades ago. She called the Info-Crime line and came in to meet with us.

"We'll be recording this session," Ryan said to her across the conference room table. "Are you okay with that?"

Fair-haired with a toned figure, Jennie had the typical girl-next-door quality that inspired trust. "Sure."

Ryan began. "Jennie, we understand that you used to babysit Vicky Johnson about twenty years ago."

She smiled briefly. "Yes. I loved babysitting Vicky. She was such a sweet child. I'm so sorry about what happened to her."

"What made you decide to come in for an interview?"

"I saw the Cinderella video the police put out. It tore me apart." Her eyes glistened with tears. "After I called the Info-

Crime line and spoke with Amber, she persuaded me to come forward and tell the police what I knew. That's why I'm here."

Ryan gave me a subtle nod of approval, then glanced at the notes on his phone. "Jennie, you told Amber that you live across the bridge in Candiac. Is that where you were living when you were babysitting Vicky?"

"No, we lived a short distance from Vicky's house then. My parents were friends with Vicky's parents."

The same positive vibes emanated from Jennie's voice now as when I first spoke with her on the phone. Eager for more details, I prompted her. "You mentioned you might have information relevant to Vicky's case."

"Yes. That is, I hope so." She looked down, as if to dredge up a memory. "It happened when I was twelve. I had babysat Vicky one evening and was walking back home. I cut through the park like I usually did. That's when a man tackled me from behind. He grabbed my legs and held me down. I'll never forget how terrified I was."

Her fear was so real that I could feel the man's weight on my legs. "How did you get away from him?"

"I turned and kicked him where it hurt," Jennie said. "I broke free, but he kept chasing me. I ran like crazy. I was a distance runner in high school at the time. It saved my life." Her lips twitched. "I'm sorry. It happened so long ago, yet I get sick to my stomach whenever I think about it."

"Can you describe your attacker?" Ryan asked her.

"No, it was dark. I only know that he was strong and had a hefty build."

"How do you know this?"

"He wrapped his hands around my calves after he tackled me. Large hands go with a large body, don't they?"

Ryan took notes. "Did your parents file a police report?"

"Yes. It didn't help much because I couldn't describe my attacker. My parents were worried that he would come after me again. So was I. They drove me to and from every babysitting job after that, even if it was a short walk from home."

"Did you tell the Johnson family about your attacker?"

"My parents told them." Jennie's forehead furrowed with worry lines. "We heard Vicky disappeared days later. I think my attack was connected to her kidnapping. The timing was quite close."

"Did the police follow up with you after Vicky was abducted?"

"Yes, but I had nothing more to add."

It explained why investigators hadn't recorded her name as a witness in Vicky's file. I jumped back into the conversation. "Jennie, when did you move away from the area?"

"Not until later," she said. "I lived in absolute fear until I finished high school. I was so stressed that my parents sent me off to college in another town. After I graduated, I moved back here to be closer to my parents. When I saw Vicky's video, my fears resurfaced. I knew I had to do the right thing and call it in."

"We're glad you did," Ryan said. "Think back, Jennie. Was there anything about your attacker that might indicate he was someone you knew? A boy from school?"

"If you mean a boyfriend, the answer is no. I was young. I wasn't allowed to date yet."

"Had anyone threatened you at the time for one reason or another?"

"No."

"Is there anything else about your attacker that you can tell us? Did he speak to you at all?"

Jennie's eyes flickered. "Yes, he did. I almost forgot. After I broke free and ran away, he shouted, 'Hey, honey, stop! I won't hurt you.' I ran even faster." She let out a nervous giggle.

I suppressed a shudder. The attacker had called her *honey*. The man who'd killed my parents had called me honey too.

After Jennie left, Ryan and I remained in the conference room.

"Jennie said her attacker had large hands," Ryan said. "It doesn't sound like Tony. He's on the thin side."

I shared my suspicions. "It's quite the coincidence that Jennie's attacker called her *honey*. He could be the same man who killed my parents and tried to kidnap me."

He gave me a doubtful look. "You're grasping at straws."

"What do you mean?"

"Lots of men call women *honey*."

"Lots of men don't try to kidnap little girls and attack female teens in the same geographic area and in the same time span," I blurted. My tone sounded brusque, even to me.

"We're butting heads over theories again. What we need are concrete leads." He stood up.

I wasn't going to let him off so easy. "Wait. The other day at the diner, before you... Anyway, you were starting to say something about connecting the dots between my impressions and aspects of the crimes we're investigating."

"So?"

"What did you mean?"

Ryan took his time to answer. "You told me you don't always understand what you experience at first. I'd like you to share your insights with me anyway, no matter how crazy they might seem to you."

"What persuaded you about the value of my...um...input?"

"The other night when I took the phone out of your hand, you went on about a car crash." He sighed. "It was my father. He died in a car accident."

I didn't reveal that the lieutenant had already told me about the accident. "I'm so sorry."

Ryan deflected my sympathy with a flick of his wrist. "Don't be. He was an alcoholic. He crashed his car into a pole one night and died instantly." He gathered his things and walked out without another word.

~

An update on Lily DeLuca arrived in the afternoon. Police officers confirmed that the seven-year-old student hadn't been physically harmed. She'd slipped out of the school on her own and hadn't been lured away by a stranger.

News about Tony Bruneau arrived, but it was far from favorable. An anonymous source called 9-1-1 to say that he'd been found unconscious and partially hidden under bags of trash in an alley. According to the police report, he'd suffered a vicious beating days earlier and was now in the hospital.

"It confirms the insight I had when we visited Tony's apartment," I said to Ryan. "It had been haunting me ever since."

"You were right about that one," he said, nodding his approval. "Tony's bad luck could mean he fell victim to a shady drug dealer or thugs. Another reason for sending him back to jail."

"Did the police find his puppy?"

"Their report made no mention of it. I wouldn't put it past Tony to have tried to trade the puppy for drugs. There's only one way to find out."

29

At the hospital the next day, Ryan asked the doctor for permission to question Tony Bruneau. Even if Lily DeLuca had been found safe, Ryan remained suspicious about Tony. He believed that the ex-con had tried to entice another student away from Blessed Mary Elementary School the other day by using his puppy as bait.

The doctor initially refused our request, then relented when Ryan stressed the importance of the case we were working on. "You have two minutes," he said, leaving us at Tony's bedside.

Tony had suffered fractured ribs, a broken arm, and numerous cuts across his face and body. Barely out of a coma, most of his body was bandaged and his bruised eyes were swollen and closed.

Ryan leaned over him. "Tony, this is Detective Ryan Baxter. Can you hear me?"

Tony partially opened his eyes and strained to focus. "Yeah."

"You were beaten up. Do you know who did this?"

"Yeah, but I wouldn't want him to come over and finish the job." Tony grinned. Two of his front teeth had been knocked out.

"Was it a drug deal gone bad?"

He cleared his throat. "Sort of. I offered the guy my puppy. He laughed at me. He said he didn't need another mouth to feed. I guess he didn't like it when I told him where to go."

"What happened to the puppy?" I asked.

"I don't know," Tony said. "I blacked out after the first punch."

Ryan went straight to the point. "We received statements from witnesses who saw you hanging around a couple of schoolyards recently."

"It wasn't me." He coughed.

"Students identified you and your dog," Ryan said, playing up the witness reports.

Tony tried to adjust his position in bed but couldn't move. "We're not in court. I don't have to say another word."

"Maybe you'd prefer answering to your parole officer instead."

"Don't threaten me with that crap. I have to answer to him anyway."

"It's a simple question. Did you speak with students in schoolyards recently?"

"I'm tired. Go away."

Ryan persisted. "We found your photo collection. Pics of you getting cozy with kids at camp."

"Oh, hell," Tony groaned. "It's not a crime to hug a child. Besides, that's old news."

"You want more recent news? How about the photos you took of kids at St. Paul Elementary School?"

"I'm done. Get out of here before I complain about police harassment." Tony closed his eyes.

Ryan turned to me. "We're wasting our time. Let's go."

On the drive back to the station, Ryan and I agreed that we had no solid evidence to pin on any of our three suspects in the Vicky Johnson case. Yet Ryan insisted on labeling Tony Bruneau as the most feasible.

I disagreed. "You honestly believe Tony kidnapped Vicky Johnson. Why?"

"Old habits die hard," Ryan said. "And now Miss Foley at St. Paul Elementary School identified Tony, even though he denied that he recently tried to chat it up with students there."

"True, but Tony wasn't the man who called the Info-Crime line and threatened me. He was unconscious in an alley at the time."

"Okay, Tony might be in the clear as far as that caller goes. I'm keeping him on my black list anyway. He's still trying to bait young kids. Who's to say he's not responsible for other abductions?"

"What happened to your argument about having solid evidence?"

Ryan steered the car into the passing lane. "As much as I hate to admit it, my gut feelings are winning out right now."

Although I admired his passing reference to intuition, our debate was getting us nowhere. I took the focus off Tony. "We issued a press release for the Cinderella case, then the media ran a video about it. There must be something else we can do to get Vicky's abductor—and my parents' killer—to surface again."

"We need a new tactic to trap him."

"How about a different slant in a new press release? Like a message that would attract his attention."

Ryan's face lit up. "Investigators used one technique before with a level of success. They issued a press release that contained a message to bluff the perp into believing the police had new evidence."

"To trip him up," I said.

"Exactly. We can announce that investigators have new

evidence and are close to solving the Cinderella case. Make the perp think we have another suspect lined up."

"If we draw the spotlight away from him, he might even resent it." I laughed.

Ryan smiled. "Totally. The message has to be strong enough to tick him off so that he'll confront us."

I recalled Laura's comment about crushing an abductor's ego. "We could say he's not a serial killer...throw in other lies."

"Perfect! Let's draft up a message that'll make his head spin."

30

Our newscast aired across the media shortly after six in the evening. A spokesperson for the police told reporters that investigators were close to solving Vicky Johnson's kidnapping that occurred twenty years ago. Since the police did not believe a serial killer was involved, the public was not in danger. Their sole suspect was last seen in Montreal with a female companion assumed to be his wife. Another press release would follow within days.

"Good work," the lieutenant said to Ryan and me after we'd viewed the news clip. "I'm calling it a day. Let me know if anything develops."

Anticipating that our strategy would persuade Vicky's abductor to call the Info-Crime line again, Ryan hung around for an hour longer. The usual calls from reporters and curious individuals initially flooded in, but when no viable leads arrived, he packed it up. "Amber, call me if you hear from our suspect, no matter what time it is."

"Okay." I settled at my desk and waited.

The infrequency of incoming calls meant Nadia was also

having a quiet night. Her giggles at the other end of the floor told me she was catching up with friends on her cell phone.

The first call on the Info-Crime line came in minutes later. I pounced on it.

The disguised voice said, "Stop spreading lies about me."

He sounded similar to the other mystery caller, though voices can sound the same with a voice-changing app. I played the part of the naïve investigator. "Lies? What do you mean?"

"I'm not married. Never have been."

I remained quiet, sensing animosity building at the other end of the line. It had to be the same caller.

"Get your records straight," he said, raising his voice. "I've killed multiple people. In your books, that makes me a serial killer."

"Do you want to come in and sign a report to make it official?"

A loud sigh. "Stay out of my life, Amber."

It was the same caller!

He ranted on. "Give up this witch hunt and save that pretty face of yours. You're a born loser and always will be. You don't have a life. You don't have friends. Hell, you don't even have a real job."

He was mocking me, trying to create self-doubt in me again.

This time, I was prepared to chip away at his narcissism and self-assurance. "Do you want to know who the real loser is? It's you. You failed when you tried to kidnap me twenty years ago."

Now it was his turn to hang in silence.

Had I succeeded in muting him with the truth? Wounding his inflated ego?

I took another leap of faith and shouted, "Why did you kill my parents?"

"It was their fault!" Anger vibrated in his voice as his words picked up speed. "They gave me no choice. They would have prevented me from completing my work. Important work. I made sure it didn't happen again."

His words repulsed me. As tempted as I was to lash out at him, I refrained. I needed more information from him. "Why did you abduct Vicky Johnson?"

A pause. "Vicky was my first successful kidnapping." His tone was measured, as if he were reminiscing. "She was such a lovely princess. I saved her and set her free for eternity." He grew vindictive in the next instant. "And now they've got *you* investigating her case. You, of all people. What a joke!"

"Why are you so cynical? You called and told us yourself that we should search for Vicky's body in Larkland Park."

I detected a brief intake of air on the phone, then silence. Had I unnerved him again?

No. His reaction could only mean one thing: He was astounded that we'd found out about Larkland Park. It confirmed our suspicions that a snitch had handed us this solid piece of evidence in an earlier Info-Crime call.

My confidence soared. "The investigators are raking through Larkland Park as we speak. Go and see for yourself if you don't believe me."

He hastily recovered. "Haven't you ever heard of fake tips? Any fool could have made that call and given you false information. You're wasting your time."

"I doubt it. That lead will take us straight to you."

He chuckled. "What the hell makes you so sure you can find me?"

"We flushed you out of the gutter to make this call, didn't we?"

A quick change of topic. "There are other victims," he said. "There will be more of them soon. Very soon."

Anger surged inside me. "We're going to find you and see you rot in jail!"

His voice deepened with rage and he blasted, "Not if I get to you first!"

The line went dead.

The danger I'd sensed was far more threatening this time

than in our previous conversation. I panted for air and gripped the crystal in my pocket.

Chatter reached me from the outer office. Nadia was still yakking with friends and oblivious to the verbal confrontation I'd had with a killer seconds ago.

I pondered my next move. There was no rush to contact Ryan and the lieutenant. The Info-Crime call was recorded. They could listen to it tomorrow. The caller had likely used a burner phone, so the police couldn't trace the call anyway.

My worst fear was that Uncle Ted might learn about this call and remove me from the job in an effort to protect me. I couldn't risk that happening, especially now that I was making headway in baiting the killer, a man who admitted moments ago that he'd murdered my parents.

I refused to give up. I was too close to seeing justice done.

I knew what I had to do.

No one would stop me this time.

31

After my nerve-racking conversation with the self-professed killer last night, subsequent calls to the Info-Crime line produced nothing except pranksters looking for a chance to shine. Since I'd put in extra hours at the station, I took time off work the next morning.

Constantly at the back of my mind were Laura's comments about abductors and how they revisit sites where they committed crimes. Their aim was to regenerate the excitement they'd felt when they carried out their monstrous acts. By doing so, they let their egos overtake any common sense.

I had a strong suspicion that my parents' home was on the killer's list of places to revisit. It was a gruesome thought, but the double murder he committed there would provide him with twice the excitement. My reason for wanting to visit my old home today was to see if I could stir up psychic readings about the crime and the criminal.

Lucky for me, the tenants had moved out days before their lease expired. Aunt Elaine had hired professional cleaners to go through the place yesterday, so I expected that the house would be in great shape.

As I drove down the familiar street, my former home loomed ahead. It was newly built when my parents moved in a year before I was born. This was the home where Mom or Dad tucked me in bed every night, where I played with my toys and looked at picture books, where I felt safe and loved. Returning to a house that I hadn't had a chance to say goodbye to twenty years earlier, let alone to my parents on our last day together, was something else.

My heart picked up speed as I fingered my house keys. Would I pick up the diverse emotions of everyone who'd lived there through the years? Or would I be able to zoom in on the embedded and loving emotions of my parents?

I unlocked the front door and stepped inside. I instantly sensed a warm rush. It was a welcoming sensation, one that is usually accompanied by hugs and kisses from family members.

Except no one was there.

I crossed the foyer and entered the living room. New draperies hung there but the room was empty. Across the floor was the dining room. It was empty too, yet the space stirred up childhood memories of happy family gatherings.

I moved along the hallway to the expansive kitchen. Deep sadness permeated the air. No surprise there. It had been a crime scene, the exact spot where my father had been killed. I blinked away tears that threatened to spill.

The white marble-topped island sat on dark oak floors that had retained most of its high sheen. The wood cabinets still held their varnish in the light. The walls, though, could use a touch of paint to brighten things up. Regardless, I absorbed the familiarity of it all with a sense of nostalgia.

I switched my focus to the sliding patio door leading to the backyard and froze. It was partially open. The cleaners had probably forgotten to shut it. Thankfully the outer screen door was locked. On the other hand, it didn't matter. Anyone could have easily cut through the screen, then flipped the small latch on the inside and entered, like the killer had done that fateful night.

I closed the sliding door and locked it. I walked back to the island and placed a hand on it as I examined the tile flooring.

Gunshots shattered the air!

Blood spatter hit the walls!

Screams echoed throughout the house!

The rapid impressions kept coming, and it was all I could do to block them from my mind. I jerked my hand off the island. Panting, I fought to catch my breath. I slipped a hand into my jacket and clasped the crystal.

Though my breathing returned to normal, the nerves in my body still prickled as I climbed the wood staircase to the second floor. I didn't know what to expect. To carry out the real purpose of my visit, I would have turned right at the landing and headed straight for my old bedroom. Instead I opened the double doors on the left that led to my parents' former bedroom.

The room was empty.

An overwhelming sense of loss overcame me, and I struggled to fight back the tears. My mother had been murdered here. A fragrant whiff of her perfume reached me. I accepted it as another perception, a gentle and loving one this time.

After a quick look in the adjoining bathroom, I made my way along the hallway. I passed the empty guest bedroom but stopped at the entrance to the TV room. My father's bulky leather armchair had drawn me to it. I figured the armchair hadn't been sold and was too heavy to carry to the basement, so Aunt Elaine had decided to leave it here.

I touched the back of the chair, now soft and worn with age. As an eager four-year-old, I'd sat on my father's lap in this chair while he read me fairy tales before bedtime. The flashback sent a pang of sorrow through me.

No time for tears, I told myself. I dashed to my childhood

bedroom at the farthest end of the floor. This room was bare, except for a new set of horizontal wood blinds.

I opened the closet door. The stencils of cute animals in vibrant colors that my father had applied along the bottom of the walls were still there. They were innocent in their appeal, yet they concealed a dark secret. The stencils camouflaged the panel behind which I'd hidden while a stranger murdered my parents.

I stepped into the closet and leaned over. I ran my hand along the stencils and felt a seam in the wall. The secret panel door! The surface of the panel was smooth and flat, which meant the knob, which was a bear's wood nose, was missing.

A memory emerged. Hiding behind the panel from the intruder that terrible night, I'd peeped through the tiny hole where the knob had once been and...

The night-light in my room cast a faint glow on the man. He was standing and wiping his sweaty face with a gloved hand... The man shouted more bad words and threw something hard against the panel door before he ran out of the room.

I tried to capture more aspects of the memory, but a sudden wave of hostility bombarded me, destroying my efforts. I jolted upright, banging my head against the top shelf, and stumbled backwards out of the closet.

I caught my balance and raced down the stairs to the unfinished basement. Aunt Elaine might have stored my old furniture in the basement. I had to find that wood knob!

White sheets covered two pieces of furniture tucked in a corner of the basement. I pulled one of the sheets off and discovered the four-drawer dresser that had held my clothes decades earlier. An assortment of toy animals had sat on the top of this dresser. Where were they now?

I opened each drawer. Empty.

I removed the second white sheet to reveal a short bookshelf that had housed my storybooks, crayons, and puzzles. It was empty. My aunt had probably sold off the rest of the furniture and moved these pieces to the basement after she'd unsuccessfully tried to sell the house.

Two dusty storage bins were stacked nearby. I took one down and removed the lid. My toy animals! Two brown bears, a yellow duck, a black puppy, and a baby elephant. I recognized the larger bear. I'd named it Coco. It had been my favorite. I'd received so many other stuffed animals in subsequent years that I'd forgotten all about these. I removed the toys, one by one. The wood knob wasn't there.

I reached for the second bin. It contained my old jigsaw puzzles, fairy-tale books, children's crayons, and smaller toys. I removed them all and peered at the bottom. Not there either. I put everything back in place.

There was only one option left.

I dashed up the stairs, across the foyer, and out of the house. My hands trembled so much that I had a hard time locking the front door.

I drove to my aunt's house with one purpose in mind: to find the clue that would reveal my parents' killer.

32

Aunt Elaine put her baking on hold and led the way down the steps to the basement. "Why do you want to find your blue butterfly barrettes after all these years?"

"I guess I'm feeling a little nostalgic," I said. "I thought they might have gotten mixed up with my toys."

She reached for a large cardboard box marked *Toys* from a pile along a wall and set it down. "These are the items we removed from your parents' home, except for a few toys that we'd left behind with bedroom furniture for the real estate showings. When the house didn't sell, I stored the remaining items over there in the basement."

"Uh-huh." I said nothing about having visited the old house. The last thing I needed was more questions. I opened the box. Each item was wrapped in tissue paper. "Oh. This could take a while."

When I didn't offer more details, Aunt Elaine said, "I'll leave you to it, then. I have to put a pie in the oven." She went back upstairs.

I dug into my pocket and pulled on a pair of thin vinyl gloves. I removed all the dolls, books, stuffed animals, and other toys before I found my target at the bottom of the box. Not the pair of blue barrettes. Those had probably been lost in the move here long ago. What I grabbed was the bear's wood nose that the killer had wrenched off the secret panel in my childhood closet.

I dropped it into the plastic evidence bag that I'd tucked in my handbag earlier. "Gotcha!" I whispered.

Ryan rose from his chair as soon as I entered our quasi office, his face taut with anger. "I listened to the call you took on the Info-Crime line last night. Why the hell didn't you tell me about it?"

I sat down at my desk. "What good would it have done? You told me that criminals use burner phones, so you couldn't have traced the call anyway."

"That's not the point. The caller intimidated you. Your life could have been in danger."

"So? What would you have done? Assigned protection to escort me home and back?"

He calmed down and pulled up a chair. "We work as a team, Amber. You have to respect that trust between us."

"I do. Here's proof that I do." I handed him the evidence bag containing the wood knob.

Ryan peered at it. "What is it?"

"A bear's wood nose. I found it in a toy box at my aunt's house. It's evidence from the night my parents were murdered."

"Evidence?"

"The wood knob was secured to a secret panel in my bedroom closet. It was the panel I hid behind when I heard the gunshots. The killer yanked the knob out when he tried to get to me, then threw it against the panel before he ran off."

"How did you know it was at your aunt's house?"

I prepared myself for a furious reaction. "I went looking for it at my old house first. It wasn't there."

Ryan jolted upright. "You did *what*? That's exactly what I mean! You can't be running off on your own like that. You should have told me what you had planned."

"I don't mean to be rude, but it is my house. Besides, what was the danger of going there in broad daylight? Don't you ever get a hunch and have to follow it through right away?"

"It's not the same. The killer's been shadowing you. He could have followed you there."

"Well, he didn't, did he?"

He grimaced. "For all we know."

The lieutenant's voice reached us. He was speaking with staff members in the outer office.

I lowered my voice. "I don't want the lieutenant to know about my visit to the old house. He might get upset, and I don't want to lose my job. My parents' case is the most important thing to me."

Ryan wasn't buying it. "You should have told me about your plans anyway."

"You would have stopped me."

"Maybe. Maybe not."

"Please, Ryan. We're so close to catching the killer. I had a flashback of him—a real memory this time—when I visited the old house. I can't describe him, but I'm certain he's the same caller I spoke with before."

He pondered my request for a long moment. "Okay, I won't tell the lieutenant. I owe you one for having saved my life. Now we're even." As he relaxed, a smile crept onto his lips. "I have to say, looking for that knob was a pretty clever move."

"To be honest, it was my last chance. The killer's fingerprints or DNA could be on that knob."

"Sounds promising. I'll ask for an analysis from forensics." He paused. "By the way, Kim Barley came through for us. She's sitting with our sketch artist right now. We should have a description of Lorne Tugg by the end of the day."

"That's good news. Kim will be hugging her grandkids more tightly from now on."

"I'm sure she will." He stood up and was about to leave when his phone rang. As he listened to the caller, unease strained his expression. "Yes, we interviewed him recently about a case. I see. Thanks for letting me know." He ended the call and stared at me.

"What's wrong?"

"A colleague in homicide found my business card in Theo's possession. His mother had filed a missing persons report with the police a couple of days ago." He choked up. "A passerby discovered the boy's body under bushes near the apartment building he shared with his mother."

33

———————

George Simon was the last person I expected to see at the police station later this morning. He didn't arrive empty-handed either.

After Ryan and I invited him to take a seat in the conference room, George placed a photo on the table. It was a shot of him standing beside his mother who was propped up by pillows in a hospital bed.

Ryan picked up the photo. "Where was this taken?"

"At the hospital," George said.

"Where did you get the photo?"

"In my mother's photo album. It proves I was with her the night you said the Vicky girl was kidnapped."

The photo album. It explained my whim to say hello to his mother the last time we dropped in on George.

Ryan asked, "Who took the photo?"

"A nurse," George said. "She used my old digital camera."

"You brought your camera to the hospital?"

"Yes. It's the only way I could create memories for my mother all these years. It helps her to remember things."

Ryan checked the timestamp on the back of the photo. "It was taken around eight o'clock."

"It's my alibi." George raised his chin. "Now you guys can finally get off my back."

"Can we hang onto this photo?"

"Yes. I don't need it. I have my mother. That's all that counts."

Ryan set the photo on the table. "You're not in the clear yet. What's your alibi for the rest of the night?"

George folded his arms and stuck out his chin. "I drove back home. Where else would I go?"

I picked up the photo and got an impression of a noisy place with lots of men—possibly a bar. "Did you go out to meet friends for a drink?"

George stared at me as if I'd slapped him in the face. "What if I did? Is it a crime?"

"Your friends might be your alibi, at least for part of the night," Ryan said. "Care to give us some names?"

"I can't win with you guys. Why do I bother?" George jumped out of his chair and thundered out of the room.

I stood up, ready to pursue him.

Ryan placed a hand on my arm. "Let him go, Amber. He won't say anything more."

I told him what I'd gathered from George's photo. "He's hiding something. Why wouldn't he tell us where he went and who he was with?"

"It would only account for a few hours anyway. He had lots of time later that night to kidnap Vicky Johnson. I'm not writing him off yet."

"Do you think George's photo is valid?" I handed it to him.

He inspected the back again. "The timestamp looks legit." He placed the photo on the table. "Did you get any other vibes from him?"

"If you want me to tell you that he's Vicky's killer, I can't.

Sorry. Regardless, I think we can eliminate one of our suspects by now. Tony Bruneau."

"Okay. We're down to George Simon and Lorne Tugg. One of them contacted you last night. We have to find a way to snag him the next time he calls. Perps like him clamor for attention."

"I'm counting on it." An image of my toy animals at the old house popped into my head. "I have an idea, but you might not go for it."

Ryan gave me a wary look. "I don't like the sound of this."

"We can't wait for forensics to analyze the prints and DNA on the bear knob. We have to move fast if we want to catch the killer. I have a sure way to trap him."

"What are you suggesting?"

I told him about my plan.

His eyes went wide. "Are you kidding? You want to put yourself up as bait?"

"You got it."

"Your idea is feasible. You might be the only one who can draw him out."

"So you agree with my plan?"

Ryan dodged the question. "From your last conversation with him, his behavior was a lot more aggressive."

"So?"

"I can't accept your plan, Amber. It's way too risky. He'll try to finish you off at the first opportunity he gets."

"We have no choice. Time is running out. We have to be ready for the next time he calls."

"Trust me, the lieutenant won't agree to it," he said with conviction.

I used the same tactic as I'd done once before. "You won't know for sure until you ask him."

He let out a heavy sigh. "Okay, but I'm telling you, it's extremely dangerous."

"It's a chance I'm willing to take."

34

After Ryan and I worked on a strategic plan to reel in the killer, we presented it to Lieutenant Payton for his approval. I crossed my fingers for a positive response. As dangerous as our plan was, it would bring us much closer to catching an evasive predator.

The lieutenant listened patiently to Ryan, but deepening creases along his brow told me he was troubled. It was clear he was considering my welfare and the anxiety that this scheme might cause my family, especially if Uncle Ted found out about it.

After we were done, the lieutenant spoke. "Amber, I think you know why I'm hesitant about agreeing to this plan."

Though I would have appreciated his concern at any other time, our proposal demanded unwavering boldness and strategic savvy if we expected to lure our target. "I know you're worried about my safety, but I'm willing to take the risk." I waited, hoping that he wouldn't reveal my family secret.

The silence seemed to drag on forever.

"Fine. On one condition." The lieutenant raised a forefinger.

"Wait for police backup before you plunge headfirst into a snake-filled pit."

Ryan nervously tapped his fingers on my desk while we sat waiting. For the third time this evening, he said, "I have no intention of losing sight of you once our plan gets underway. Remember that."

I had my own qualms. "It's seven thirty. What if he doesn't call? Why is he torturing us like this?"

"Don't worry, he'll call. He wants to find out what we're up to."

"No, he just wants another opportunity to criticize me or threaten me to get off the case," I said, trying to sound light-hearted, even though my nerves were on edge.

The phone rang.

Ryan leaned forward.

I knew it was the killer before his words reached me. As Ryan had predicted, the mystery man's curiosity had prompted him to call back.

I hit the speakerphone button.

"You're so boringly obvious, Amber," the disguised voice said. "You couldn't stay away from the old house, could you? You're still living in the past with all those ghosts. Maybe that's where you belong. In the past." He released a light chuckle.

Clutching the crystal in my pocket, I spoke with quiet confidence. "You don't have to use the voice-changing app any longer. I know who you are. And I know what you look like."

"You're lying."

"I have proof."

"You're bluffing. How dare you try to deceive me like this?"

I remained silent. He wanted information, and I intended to make him beg for it.

He went on. "Why did you visit the old house anyway? It's empty, except for curtains and a few pieces of furniture."

He'd been inside the house!

I pretended not to notice and hid the astonishment in my voice. "I wanted to say goodbye to it. I never had the opportunity."

"You expect me to buy that excuse?" he scoffed. "You could have done that years ago. Why did you go there?"

"I already told you."

"Then you're more incompetent than I thought. Why do I bother to call—"

"Wait!" I needed to keep him talking. "I went to my aunt's house afterward."

"I know. I followed you there." He sighed. "This is getting really boring. Why do I waste my precious time?"

"Hold on! Okay, I'll tell you the truth. I went to my aunt's place to look through my old toy box. I wanted to find a nanny cam that my parents had placed inside a stuffed animal. You know, those tiny spy cameras that parents hide in their child's bedroom to make sure they're safe."

"Honey, I wasn't born yesterday. I can tell when someone is trying to scam me."

I ignored him and continued to play the game to gain his trust, the way he tricked his victims to trust him. "You know what puzzles me? I couldn't find the nanny cam in the toys my aunt had stored away. I wanted to find it and pull out the SD card so that I could watch the video of you prowling around in my old bedroom. Anyway, it doesn't matter. I'm sure I'll find it eventually, and when I do, you'll be history."

Dead silence at the other end of the line.

I hardened my tone. "Oh. One more thing. I'm bringing a few items to the old house tonight, and I'll be moving in permanently on the weekend."

The line went dead.

A smile spread across Ryan's face. "Fantastic work, Amber. I enjoyed how speechless he got when you mentioned the nanny cam."

"I burst his ego by pointing out his mistake," I said. "It stirred up doubts in him about a detail he might have missed."

"What's important is that he took the bait. I'll alert the surveillance team to get ready to move in. Let's go."

We were confident that the killer would immediately drive to the old house. Since he'd clearly found a way to get inside before, he would head directly for the stuffed animals stored in the basement. I envisioned him frantically searching for the fake nanny cam that our tech colleague had hidden inside one of the toys earlier. When he'd dart back out, the police would nab him.

With a surveillance team in place, Ryan watched the action unfold from a distance. As planned, I drove to the house with Joe, an undercover cop who acted as my "friend." We put on a performance of friendly banter and laughter as we carried boxes into the house.

Once we were inside, I locked the front door.

"Let's go through the motions in case our target is casing the house," Joe said. "We'll walk around the main floor first, as if you're showing me around."

He followed me into the kitchen. The sliding door was closed and locked this time, but it didn't mean anything. If the killer had trespassed before, he'd trespass again.

My attention was drawn to the island in the middle of the kitchen. A new item had been added since my last visit. A bowl of red apples!

My heart hammered in my chest. "Joe," I whispered, "did you or another officer put that bowl of apples on the counter?"

"They did a sweep of the house, but I can verify that for you." He took out his phone. After a brief conversation with someone at headquarters, he hung up. "They'll call me back to confirm one way or the other."

Joe's words didn't reassure me. The bowl of apples in the kitchen wasn't a coincidence. Other than Laura and me, only the killer knew what the red apples signified.

"In the meantime, let's go upstairs," Joe said.

I led the way, eager to see if anything else had changed since my last visit.

Joe entered my parents' bedroom and turned on the light. When his phone rang, he retrieved it and took the call.

On impulse, I deviated to the right and hurried to my old bedroom. I flicked on the light.

The room was empty, with one exception. A white plastic bag sat on the floor next to the closet, its bumpy shape betraying its furry toy contents. Two tiny blue items were inserted into the plastic: two butterfly barrettes. They were identical to the pair I'd worn as a young girl.

My pulse accelerated.

The killer was here! In this house!

A hard object clattered to the floor in my parents' bedroom, then a heavy thud.

The taste of bile rose in my throat.

My phone rang. I fumbled to dig it out of my pocket and almost dropped it.

It was Ryan. "Amber, get out of the house! Now!" He sounded out of breath, as if he were running.

The floor creaked behind me. I spun around.

A hefty, unshaven man in jeans and a pullover snatched the phone out of my hand and cut off the call. "Honey, you won't be needing this." He flung it across the floor.

That gruff voice. How could I forget it? It was the same voice I'd heard the night my parents were killed.

The sight of his broad face, massive chest, and dark sunken eyes under a tuft of white hair sent chills through me. "Lorne Tugg." My words were barely audible.

"If you insist," he sneered.

Fear glued me to the spot. I was no match for this man built like a brick barricade. There was nothing in the room that I could use as a weapon to defend myself against him either.

He surveyed the room with admiration, as if he were recalling his initial visit here. "I was standing in this spot twenty years ago when I came for you. You would have been my first."

He was blocking my path to the door. I stepped back, putting space between us, and attacked him in the only way I could. "You murdered my parents!"

"Honey, I couldn't compete with them for your attention. Besides, they were in the way. They were preventing me from saving you." His words were emotionless, like the dull look in his eyes.

The treacherous evil in this man abruptly swept over me like a tidal wave of malice, materializing as a tightness in my chest. I was so distraught that I couldn't speak.

Lorne grinned. "You were a special child. I'm so sorry we missed out on being together during your early years. But all is not lost. After I leave here, I can revisit your old bedroom anytime I want, thanks to the nanny cam in one of those toys." He motioned to the plastic bag. "It's too bad you won't be alive to review the other cases."

I found my voice and prodded him on. "What other cases?"

"There are as many victims as there are fairy tales. Unfortunately, we don't have time to get into the details."

He was bragging about himself again. Good. His reference to fairy tales made me sick to my stomach. Yet as nauseous and scared as I felt in his presence, I had to urge him on and stall for time. "There's something I need to know. Why did you wait to return Vicky Johnson's missing slipper until now?"

"Ah, yes. The Cinderella case." Lorne raised his chin for dramatic effect, as if I were a fan of his work. "I'm somewhat...What's the word you would use? Yes, sentimental. I'm sentimental about the children I pick and how I honor them. You see, this week is the twentieth anniversary of Vicky's abduction. I love celebrations and wanted to share my joy with Vicky's family. Don't you like celebrations?"

"You're sick."

He shrugged. "I've had better days."

I racked my brain for a way to keep him talking about

himself. "Does this mean you're done? No more child abductions?"

He wrinkled his nose. "Abduction is such an ugly word. Let's use *salvation* instead."

I fought the queasiness mounting inside me. "Salvation?"

"Obviously," Lorne said. "Someone had to save those poor innocent children. I thought about my ambitious goals and realized that I couldn't do it alone. It was an enormous task. The answer was to train others who shared my ideals. They helped me to achieve what I set out to do."

"What do you give them in return?"

"Nothing but gratitude. It's a matter of trust. By forming a hierarchy of loyal subjects, I can now ensure that my legacy continues."

"Legacy? To what purpose?"

His flinty stare pierced my heart like a knife. "For recognition, of course. It's the only thing that counts. The rest of the world will soon acknowledge me. I'll be legendary, like Ted Bundy."

It was outrageous. He ranked himself among the most notorious serial killers of the 1970s, devious predators that targeted the innocent. "Do you actually expect anyone to congratulate you for kidnapping and murdering children?"

"Tsk-tsk. Such ugly words." Lorne scowled at me. "Don't you see, Amber? I needed to save them from this corrupt world. Even you can understand that, can't you?"

His malevolence had grown into a darkness that I was failing to handle. Desperation seized me. Where was Ryan? The surveillance team?

Grasping at ideas, I continued to stall him. "You must be very intelligent to have evaded the police all these years. How did you manage to fly under the radar for so long?"

"You know me as Lorne Tugg, but I used other pseudonyms. Since you've come this far, I'll tell you my real name. You should know who I am before I kill you." He chuckled. "Soon everyone will know my name and I'll be famous."

I egged him on. "Famous? For a handful of kidnappings and murders? Hah! Others in your league have achieved bigger news headlines than that."

Lorne glared at me. "Weren't you listening? I am unique in my quest. I train other budding saviors who are devoted to my cause."

My stomach churned at the idea of cloned predators like him. "Saviors? You teach them how to manipulate and entice children. How to abuse them. How to make sure the children don't live to tell."

His eyes blazed. "You're wrong. I've built an empire! A legacy! My team worships me!"

"You're insane!"

The veins in his neck bulged. "You just spoke your last words!" He pounced on me and grasped my neck with his large hands.

Children—dozens of them—screaming in terror as they ran through the woods. He was chasing them!

I used both hands to break his grip on me, but it was useless. I began to see spots. I was going to pass out within seconds. Gasping for air, I turned my head to the side and drew in a tiny breath of air. I had one last chance to save myself.

I seized the jagged crystal from my pocket and jabbed it hard into his left eye.

Lorne howled in pain and reeled backward. His hands flew to his face.

I scrambled toward the doorway.

He tackled me, and we both hit the floor. "You won't get away from me this time." Keeping his weight on me, he grabbed me firmly by the neck again.

My vision began to fade. The distant sound of breaking glass...

Lorne stopped. "What the hell—"

Footsteps pounded up the stairs.

Ryan tore in and seized Lorne by the hair, landing several punches to his face. Two undercover police officers rushed in and helped to restrain and handcuff Lorne.

I scrambled to my feet and gulped air into my lungs. I leaned against the wall, thankful that the ordeal was over.

As the police officers steered Lorne out of the room, he stopped before me, his white hair disheveled, blood dripping down his face. "Honey, it's not over yet. The others will be waiting for you."

"When karma comes back to punch you in the face again," I said with confidence, "I'll be there in case it needs help."

"Does Chief Tremblay know that his niece is playing dangerous mind games?" Lorne's mouth twisted in a hideous smirk as the officers yanked him into the hallway.

Ryan placed his hands on my shoulders. "Amber, are you okay?"

I met his troubled gaze. "I will be."

He slowly let his hands fall to his sides. "You took a gigantic risk. I shouldn't have agreed to—"

"It was the only way to flush him out. We had no choice." I rubbed my neck, easing the tightness.

"We should get you the hospital and have the doctor examine you."

"No need. I'll be fine. What took you so long to get here anyway?"

"We tried to get in through the front door, but it was locked. We broke in through the back door. Don't worry, we'll pay for the damages."

"You bet you will." I managed a weak smile.

Ryan gave me another uneasy look. "What Lorne said about your relation to Chief Tremblay... Is that true?"

"Yes. Uncle Ted and Aunt Elaine adopted me. I didn't tell you. I wanted to prove I could do the job first."

His face registered mixed emotions, spanning from amazement to respect. "You just did." He smiled. "Let's get out of here."

I followed him down the stairs. "I thought the police had performed a sweep of the house earlier."

"They did," Ryan said over his shoulder.

"So how did Lorne get in?"

"We think he hid in a neighbor's backyard and slipped into the house through a basement window afterward. Rats like him have a way of hiding behind walls."

I knew all about hiding behind walls. "He told me his real name wasn't Lorne Tugg."

"What is it?"

"He didn't say."

"What did he mean by, 'the others will be waiting for you'?"

I shivered involuntarily. "There are many more like him out there."

EPILOGUE

Lorne Tugg admitted to using Larry Tuft among his numerous aliases but revealed no other names to police investigators. However, he did confess that his real name was Leonard Trover. That he would use LT—the same initials as his real name—for his aliases was odd, if not conceited. It was just one of the head games he played with police.

As Leonard Trover, he'd spent a short time in jail for minor assault offenses and had his record purged afterward. A clean slate triggered his killing spree. Investigators had interviewed him as Lawrence Townsend, the man in Michael Elliott's unsourced video. Although he'd told them he didn't own a truck at the time, he now admitted he'd lied. Sort of. He'd registered the truck under another LT alias. For a good cause, he said. He delivered toys at Christmas to welfare families with young kids.

Ryan and I agreed we'd use the abbreviated LT when referring to the serial killer. It robbed him of a human identity, yet it was nothing compared to the innocent lives he'd stolen from families.

A lab test matched LT's DNA to the DNA found on the

slipper left on the Johnsons' porch, a sign that he'd grown either sloppy or overconfident. Faced with solid evidence against him, LT confessed that he'd kidnapped Vicky from her bedroom. He'd kept her in a second storage unit that he'd leased under the alias Larry Tuft, which was how he eluded investigators. He later disposed of her body in a pine box.

Days after the police arrested LT, the QPP search team found Vicky's remains in Larkland Park. Forensics speculated that LT would have required assistance to transport the pine box into the forest a mile from the road and dig a grave several feet deep. It supported his confession that he had access to "trainees" to help him carry out his horrific deeds.

The discovery of the pine box meant that investigators continued to put LT in the public spotlight. I shuddered to think that solving more of his crimes would raise his profile to the level of his most illustrious and admired counterparts. Hadn't that been his ultimate goal all along?

As for Theo, we suspected that LT had killed the teen when he found out he'd spoken with Ryan and me. That investigation was still ongoing.

Then there was the court case for my parents. It was one thing for LT's defense lawyer to argue that the fake nanny cam hidden in my stuffed bear was inadmissible evidence. It was another to ignore LT's DNA on the knob I'd retrieved from my aunt's home. The simple act of wiping the sweat from his face before flinging the bear's wood nose at the secret panel meant LT would spend the rest of his life in jail. Traces of my parents' blood on the knob reinforced the case against him.

When police tracked down LT's address to a boarding-house, the evidence against him kept piling up. Forensics found thousands of photos of children on his computer. Each photo was labeled by name, date, and physical description. The photos of children in playgrounds, schoolyards, and in grocery carts pushed by their mothers reinforced the prosecution's case against him.

Forensics also found the photo of LT with a blonde woman. The writing on the back read *Leonard and sister Joyce at Mount Royal Park.* LT had shown this same photo to Kim Barley to imply he already had a girlfriend. A search for his sister revealed that she'd died from cancer several years after the photo had been taken.

With an attempt through his defense lawyer, LT promised to give police the names of other child molesters in exchange for a reduced jail sentence. Ryan assured me that any change to LT's jail term would never happen.

The cold case unit's task ahead was immense. From the evidence collected on LT, investigators would need to examine possible links to other cases and get in touch with the victims' families. The sketch artist's drawing of a younger and slimmer LT, obtained thanks to Kim Barley, was a timely tool that would come in handy for witness interviews.

Joe, the undercover officer, had suffered a mild concussion when LT had knocked him unconscious. He returned to duty a week later.

In the process of wrapping up loose ends, Lieutenant Payton announced that Ryan and I were now official closers of cold case files. An increased budget meant more resources were on the way.

I couldn't thank Aunt Elaine enough for having persuaded me to keep the amethyst cluster close at hand. "It saved my life," I told her when I visited her and Uncle Ted one evening.

She smiled at me. "No, dear. You did it all on your own."

Uncle Ted beamed with pride. "I knew you had it in you, Amber."

"The old crystal is evidence now, so I had to part with it," I said.

Aunt Elaine handed me a small velvet pouch. "Here's a new crystal. I bathed it in sea salt and it's ready to go."

I thanked her again and tucked it in my pocket, prepared with a safeguard for my next case.

I finally called Nicole and apologized for not getting in touch with her sooner, using a heavy workload and overtime hours as an excuse.

"No need to explain, Amber," she said. "I can see that your job is very demanding. It must help to work with an experienced detective like Ryan."

"Yes, it does." I sensed that she was curious about my relationship with him, but I wasn't about to open the door to that conversation.

We left off, promising we'd get together soon.

~

"I would have never thought that painting was such a great stress reducer," Ryan said, guiding the paintbrush over the kitchen baseboard Sunday afternoon. "Amber, can I ask you something personal?"

"Sure." My pulse quickened. The physical attraction between us was impossible to ignore, especially when he'd offered to help me get the old house ready so I could move back in. I placed dishes in the cupboards I'd painted yesterday as I anticipated his question.

He paused and glanced up at me. "Why didn't you sell this house and buy another one instead?"

My attachment to my childhood house was complicated and bittersweet. I felt a catch in my throat as I searched for the right words to express my feelings. "This home was my first love. Though I was a young child, I remember the happy memories I formed here with my parents. I wanted to build on those memories."

He smiled. "I'm sure you will."

Our eyes locked, and I knew at that moment that our unspoken attraction was mutual. Our bond was professional, not romantic, but I didn't doubt for a minute where we were headed. We just had to take things slowly.

The soothing pitter-patter of rain had a calming effect as we worked in silence. I sensed tranquility in the house. Part of it came from the satisfaction that I'd fulfilled my promise and helped bring my parents' killer to justice. In the process, I'd learned to trust my gift such that my newfound confidence brought me peace of mind.

After Ryan left, I walked over to the living room window and looked out. The afternoon shower had subsided, leaving a rainbow in its place. I took it as a sign that my parents had transformed into light and moved on to a better place.

As I would, now that I was finally home again.

ACKNOWLEDGMENTS

It should come as no surprise that my love of fairy tales at a young age inspired the writing of *The Missing Slipper*. These stories taught me how important it was to keep hope alive, no matter how difficult the path ahead might seem.

My gratitude goes out to the beta readers, proofreaders, editor, and cover designer who contributed valuable feedback to the process. I also want to thank my family and friends for their unwavering devotion and support.

A special thank you goes to readers who motivate me to keep on writing. I wouldn't be here without your interest in my work.

ABOUT THE AUTHOR

Sandra Nikolai is the author of the Megan Scott/Michael Elliott Mystery series and the Amber McNeil Mystery series. In addition to her novels, Sandra has published a string of short crime stories, garnering awards along the way.

A graduate of McGill University in Montreal, Sandra held jobs in sales, finance, and high tech before leaving the corporate world to pursue a career in writing. She likes to think that plotting a whodunit reveals the lighter—yet more mysterious—side of her persona.

Visit www.sandranikolai.com and sign up for Sandra's quarterly newsletter to get news on book releases, exclusive promotions, and other inside information. Your email address will never be shared and you can unsubscribe at any time.

You can also find Sandra on

Twitter: twitter.com/SandraNikolai

Facebook: facebook.com/SandraNikolaiAuthor

Instagram: instagram.com/sandranikolaiauthor

ALSO BY SANDRA NIKOLAI

Amber McNeil Mystery series

The Red Hoodie

Silent Night

Megan Scott/Michael Elliott Mystery series

False Impressions

Fatal Whispers

Icy Silence

Dark Deeds

Broken Trust

Cold Revenge

For more details and store links, visit Sandra's Books page on her website at www.sandranikolai.com